AF422482

DIAMONDS IN THE ROUGH

ON THE RANCH

BOOK 3

JODI PAYNE

BA TORTUGA

This is a work of fiction. Names, characters, places, and incidents either are the product of the author's imagination or are used fictitiously. Any resemblance to actual events, locales, organizations, or persons, living or dead, is entirely coincidental and beyond the intent of either the author or the publisher.

Diamonds in the Rough
Copyright © 2024 by Jodi Payne & BA Tortuga

Edited by LC Hinson

Cover illustration by AJ Corza
http://www.seeingstatic.com/
Cover content is for illustrative purposes only and any person depicted on the cover is a model.

All rights reserved. This book is licensed to the original purchaser only. Duplication or distribution via any means is illegal and a violation of international copyright law, subject to criminal prosecution and upon conviction, fines, and/or imprisonment. No part of this book may be reproduced or transmitted in any form or by any means, electronic or mechanical, including photocopying, recording, or by any information storage and retrieval system, without the written permission of the Publisher, except where permitted by law. To request permission and all other inquiries, contact Tygerseye Publishing, LLC, www. tygerseyepublishing.com

Published by Tygerseye Publishing, LLC
August 2024

DIAMONDS IN THE ROUGH

When Asher Allen heads west to become the nanny to a family in New Mexico for the summer, he's expecting three kids who've lost their parents. He's expecting to have to step in and save the day so their uncle, the cowboy who took them in, can get back to work on the family ranch. What he doesn't expect is to fall so hard for New Mexico. And for his new boss.

Sebastian Martindale is about to give up and make a run for it when Ash arrives. His niece hates him, he never gets enough sleep, and he can't juggle three small kids and the mountain of work that needs to get done. Despite his total exhaustion he's skeptical when his mom hires a nanny, but once Ash shows up, Bastian isn't sure how he'd managed without the man.

Together, Bastian and Ash have to navigate the children's grief, the first day of school, helping the kids understand they have a home right where they are, and falling for each other at the same time. Can they work it all out and polish up the diamonds in the rough they find?

As always, to our wives.

THE ON THE RANCH SERIES

Tending Tyler

Roped In

Diamonds in the Rough

These are all stand-alone novels, though some readers say it's good to read Roped In before Diamonds in the Rough.

1

Holy fuck. This place looks like a hotel.

Asher Allen drove past the rustic sign that read "Diamond M Ranch" and up the long driveway toward the main house. The closer he got, the bigger the house seemed, until he started to wonder if he was in the right place.

Two floors, a thousand windows, a picture postcard view...

Toto, we are not in Kansas anymore.

What the hell had he gotten himself into? It had been a long trip from New York, and he was not at all ready for... whatever this place was. He took a couple of pictures with his phone and texted them to his best friend Max.

ASH

Made it. This is home for the next three months. Or it's a cult. I guess we'll see.

Two stories of white plaster. Huge balconies. Three trucks in the driveway. Great big windows.

It was wild and absolutely not kid-friendly and—

A little naked red-headed boy went running across the

second-story balcony, followed by a screaming man holding a second naked little boy.

Wow.

Guess I'm in the right place after all.

He popped the trunk and pulled out his suitcase, got his backpack from the back seat, stuffed his phone in his pocket, and headed for the front steps. He hauled everything onto the first-floor porch and knocked on the door.

Then he rang the doorbell.

And then knocked again.

Asher decided the guy wasn't coming to the door if he was busy chasing naked children around upstairs, so he let himself in.

"Hello?" he called out. "It's Ash. Asher Allen. The nanny?"

A young girl with hair as black as night—Samantha, if he remembered correctly—peered at him from the top of the stairs. "Are you here to take us back to Connecticut?"

She was adorable, with big eyes, and her long hair was pulled back in a hairband. "No, I'm sorry. I'm here to help you get settled in New Mexico though. Are you Samantha?"

"Uh-huh. Uncle Bastian is going to dunk my brothers in the tub. If he can catch Will. Walt is slower."

"Maybe I can help." He left his things at the bottom of the stairs and made his way up. "Is there a trick to catching him that I should know? I bet you know all the tricks."

"I do. He likes to play freeze dance."

"Who are you talking to, girl? Is someone here?" The voice was stressed, full of a near-desperate edge.

"Asher Allen, your nanny." He climbed the rest of the stairs to meet his employer. The guy had such a great name. Sebastian. How dignified was that?

"Oh. Shit. I—" A cowboy in jeans, boots, and a soaking wet T-shirt stood there with two dripping little boys in his arms. "Hey. Bastian Martindale. I assume you been talking to my mama, Stella?"

Bastian. Okay, then. "I think so, yes. She was working with my agency. What can I do?"

"I—" The man blinked for a second. "I don't know. What *can* you do?"

"Let him take us back to Connecticut," the little girl snapped.

"Sam. You're not going anywhere."

Ash had his eyes and ears open. He knew very few details about what had happened, but he knew the family was grieving. This had to be so hard for these kids, especially Samantha, at her age.

Bastian was carrying both boys now. It seemed like that game of freeze dance wasn't going to be necessary, but he filed it away for next time.

With boys, there was always a next time.

"Bath time?"

"The water is run in the big tub. You'd think they'd like it, but they fight every inch."

"No!" one screamed.

As the other went, "No baf!"

He reached out and took one of the boys from Bastian. "What's your name?"

"I'm Will."

"Oh, you're the fast one. I've heard about you. I love a bath. You sure you don't want one? I can totally go enjoy the warm water and the toys and all instead."

Walt frowned at him, suspicious, but Will lit up. "Toyses? I play!"

"I don't know, you said no bath, but if you've changed

your mind, that's cool. You can have some bath toys." He looked at Samantha. "Help me out here; where am I going?"

"Uncle Bastian's room. He has the great big bathroom. *Great* big." Samantha rolled her eyes. "Come on. I'll show you."

She pointed an imperious finger, the other boy started struggling in the cowboy's arms, and for a second, Ash could see utter exhaustion.

"Okay, let's go." He went the way Samantha was pointing and set Will down in the tub, then turned to take—Walt? Was it Walt?—from Bastian.

"I got this." He gave Bastian a smile. "Samantha will show me where the boys' room is so I can get them in pjs. You're good. Go have a drink." He started tossing everything he could find that would float into the bathtub to be used as toys. Plastic cups, washcloths, a mostly empty shampoo bottle.

"Okay..." Bastian grabbed a towel on his way and headed out of the room with a sigh.

"He's not a dad. He's not my dad." Samantha sat on the closed commode. "Did you know my mom and dad?"

"No, but I wish I had. He's not trying to be your dad, Samantha; he's just trying to give you a safe home. I think he's new at this parenting stuff, you know?"

The boys splashed and laughed, and he managed to get Walt shampooed without the kid even really noticing. One down...

Will dumped a glass of water on his own head, cheering. "I do!"

Oh, this little boy was fearless.

"Wow, you're good at that." He quickly lathered up Will's head. "Do it again!"

"Again!" Will filled the cup and poured it over his head. "Again!"

Walt began to cry.

Oh, boy.

"You want a turn, Walt?" He grabbed another cup and put it in Walt's hands. "You can do it too." He glanced over his shoulder at Samantha. He was going to make her feel so smart and useful she didn't have time to miss Connecticut. "Are they always like this?"

"They're awful, but they're mine, so I have to keep them." She sighed, so dramatic. "There aren't any fun kids here."

He kept his hands busy with the boys while he talked with her. Finish the bath, pop the boys in pjs—had they had dinner yet? "No? What about school? That should be starting soon, right?"

"Yes!" Like it was a betrayal. "I'm running out of time!"

"Running out of time for what?" He hit the drain on the bathtub and rinsed the boys off. "Towels?"

"I'll get them. For the summer. I don't want to go to school here. I don't like it here. I won't go." She handed him towels. "I'm going back to my old house, my old school."

"Oh, I see." He understood. It wasn't something he was going to argue with her about when he'd been here five minutes. Or really, ever. He'd just have to help her like it here.

Assuming he figured out how to like it here.

Gotta love a challenge.

He took the towels and wrapped the boys in them. He picked Will up but offered Walt his hand. "Show me your room, Walt."

"Room! Room!" The little boy glanced at his sister, wide-eyed. "Sisser?"

"You have the blue room. Will has the green room." She rolled her eyes. "Not that it matters. They always end up together."

"Twins do. It's a thing." He sort of led and sort of followed Walt into a blue room and closed the door behind them, hoping that would at least slow Will down if he took off. "Pajamas..." He looked around and finally started opening dresser drawers.

"Turtle ones." Will pointed to the bed. "Turtle."

Walt went to the dresser and opened up another drawer, pulling out a pair of pajamas with moose all over them. "Dease ones."

"Okay. Perfect." Turtles for Will, moose for Walt. "You guys look great." He glanced at Samantha. "Have you all had dinner?"

"No. Everything here is hot. *Everything*."

"Eggses! Eat all the eggses!" Will cheered, and Walt climbed up on the little bed, covering his head with the blankets.

"Okay. You want eggs? I can make eggs, no problem. Walt? Are you coming?" He gave Walt's little butt a pat. Scrambled eggs were a perfectly fine dinner for his first night in town.

"Eggses. Eggses. Egg-a-ses!" Will cheered and marched to the top of the stairs, where Bastian met them.

"No boys on the stairs alone, little dude." Bastian met Samantha's eyes. "You going to eat?"

"Are you going to cook?"

Those lips tightened, and Bastian shrugged one shoulder. "Starve, then. I don't care. Stay up here with your brother."

"Fine." Samantha crossed her arms.

"Whoa, now. I can cook. No one needs to starve. Good

rule about the stairs though. You got this one? Let me grab Walt." He went back for the boy with his head still under the blanket and scooped him up. "Dinner, buddy."

Walt just snuggled right into him with a little hum, but that was it. No fight. Just a snuggle.

Poor kid. That was a little boy who wanted his mommy. Will probably did too; he just seemed better at distracting himself.

When he got to the stairs, everyone was already gone, probably on their way to the kitchen. That was quite a staring match between Bastian and Samantha. She was angry, and he was out of patience—or just plain energy—for it. He couldn't blame either of them. This was impossibly hard, incredibly unfair, and there was nothing either of them could do about it.

Well, Bastian could have refused to take the kids in, Ash supposed, but he hadn't, and something about the guy's vibe told Ash that he wouldn't have even thought about that. Bastian seemed like a family guy—his mother had set all of this up, so they must be close too.

The kitchen was tense when he walked in. Samantha was at the table with Will, and Bastian had his back turned to her, making something. Coffee?

He walked over and stood beside Bastian. "I'm sorry that I just barged into your home like that, but it seemed like you could use a minute to yourself."

"Yeah. A minute. Thanks, man. I'll get you set up with your rooms and everything here in a bit. I—Thanks for jumping in."

The kitchen door thumped open. "Boss? You need to sign off on all this sh—shtuff from the auction house."

The man who came stomping in was filthy, smelled bad, and had a voice like a foghorn.

Walt immediately started wailing, while Will launched himself toward the big guy—who had obviously been rolling in manure.

Samantha caught Will by his collar and pulled him back, which wasn't ideal but got the job done. He bounced Walt on his hip and tried not to wrinkle his nose too obviously at the stench. "Oh, good catch, Samantha."

The temptation to tell the guy that they were all standing right there, and he needn't shout was almost irresistible, but he managed for the sake of... something. Respect. Politeness. Just being too new to rock the boat yet. Something. He hadn't been here an hour and all he'd seen was chaos. The house was serene and stately on the outside, and a whirlwind of emotion and noise and... stinky on the inside.

"You know it. I took a tumble out there chasing that dinosaur chicken. Sammy, girl, you know your face is going to freeze that way?"

"Oh for... those ostriches are going to be the death of me. Wylie, this is Allen. Asher Allen. He's the guy Mama hired from back East."

"Well, Allen Asher Allen! Triple A! I'm pleased to meetcha. I need that stuff done for the auction before tomorrow, Boss. Don't forget." The big man winked at him. "Y'all need anything from town? Tacos? Beer? A pair of penguins from the zoo?"

Soap?

God, that almost came out of his mouth.

"Penwings!" Will tried to make another run for Wylie, but Samantha was on it.

"It's good to meet you, Wylie."

Do not say "coyote".

Ash was going to get in trouble here. He could feel it.

"We'll have a beer later, huh? Everyone will want to meet you. Don't forget that—"

Bastian slapped one hand on the counter. "I said I'll do it, man. Get your skanky ass out of here, or I'll tell Anna you tracked shit through her kitchen!"

Whoa.

Ash flinched and reflexively took a couple of steps backward. Walt was practically inconsolable now, crying into his shoulder. Even Will was a little wide-eyed.

Samantha huffed and shook her head like all the adults had gone crazy, and maybe they had.

And who was Anna? He was sure he'd been told Bastian lived alone.

Wylie, though, he just chuckled and shook his head. "I ain't scairt. My old lady is a paragon of womanhood. I'll bring tacos in a bit. See you later, Boss, Triple A, Sammy, lost boys."

Huh. Wylie said "ain't" and used "paragon" correctly in the same breath. This place was wild. "It's just two A's actually..." He didn't manage to get that out before Wylie closed the door.

Everyone went still in the kitchen for a second, and then Walt started wailing again. "Okay... hey, buddy. It's all good." Hopefully. Bastian needed a drink and a nap. And maybe not to have children around, but here they were. "Can I make the kids some eggs?"

"Of course. What do you need besides eggs? Cheese? Milk? The pots and pans are here." He opened up a cabinet, and the stacks of pans gleamed. Nice.

"Yes, all of those things. A mild cheese if you have one? Thank you." He turned to Samantha. "Do you guys like toast with your eggs? You want them wrapped in a tortilla? Something else?"

"No tortillas. Only my daddy ate tortillas."

Bastian took Walt from him. "Hush, pup. I got you. We'll go see the puppies after you eat, if you're nice."

Walt grabbed Bastian, leaned in and whispered, and Bastian nodded. "Sure, you can have a tortilla, pup."

Ash hid his grin and started scrambling eggs in a large bowl. "So, no spices, Samantha? What about the boys?"

"Will is no spice. Walt is a New Mexican in his soul, aren't you, pup? He likes to share chile with his tio, don't you?"

"Tio?" He found the cheese and milk, and a loaf of bread.

"It's Spanish for uncle. I'm their Tio Bastian."

"He's Uncle Bastian," Samantha insisted.

"That works too. I'm easy." And furious, but holding it in, Ash could see it.

"What's Spanish for nanny? Or... Manny?" He chuckled, pouring the eggs into the pan and listened to them sizzle. He popped in the toast for Samantha and pulled out tortillas for the boys. He'd like Will to learn to like a tortilla; it made eating so easy.

"El niñero."

Oh, okay. That was actually really pleasant to the ear.

"I speak French." Samantha shook her head. "Not Spanish."

"You can speak both." Bastian didn't sound the slightest bit worried.

"Moi aussi, Samantha. But we can learn Spanish, too. And German. And Italian also, if we want to."

He noticed then that Walt was quiet. Walt trusted Bastian. Good to know. Maybe Bastian was right about the boy being New Mexican in his soul.

"Did I tell y'all there is a new foal in the barn? She's a pretty thing. In a couple of days, we'll go see her."

"You have a foal? How cool. I've never seen one except in pictures or TV. What about you Samantha?"

"I guess I could see her. There's nothing else to do around here."

"Nope. Just miles and miles of nature." Bastian was trying not to explode—that was obvious—but the cracks were starting to show.

"Moo cows, Sisser!" Will pronounced. "Kiki and doggies and—" He looked to Bastian.

"Churro sheep and coyotes and llamas."

"Cowdodies! Aroo!"

He smiled at that because it was so adorable. Bastian had been putting in the time with these kids, despite everything. He put the eggs on plates, wrapping two up with cheese inside tortillas, and set them down on the table for the boys, then put toast on Samantha's plate.

"Do you want cheese on your eggs, Samantha?"

"Yes?" She looked so suspicious, so worried about her answer.

"Great." He added some cheese and folded the eggs around it so it would melt. "Here you go." He leaned toward her and gave her a wink. "You're allowed to like what you like."

"Yeah. I don't like spicy food. I don't like oats. I don't like it here."

Bastian sat with Walt. "You want to sit on your seat, pup? Eat some good eggs?"

Walt nodded and sat down to eat, tearing into the tortilla. Will had already finished half of his.

"What can I make for you, Bastian? Or should we have some dinner after we put the kids down and... talk a little?"

"I think you and I have to make a plan. I'll need to show you your rooms and all that. How about planning to meet post getting the twins down?"

"Sounds good. I've got this if you want to relax a little, or... go see what Wylie needed you for." Helpful. He was there to look after the kids, but also to be a help to Bastian. That's what Bastian's mother had said. *My boy needs help.*

"Perfect. I'm going to go send that information to the auction house, then we'll see the puppies, okay y'all?"

"Pees." Walt nodded, offering Bastian a smile.

This was a good start. Jumping in was somehow better than taking it slow and awkward introductions. He was here now, working already, helping where he could.

The hardest part of this job wasn't going to be two wild twin boys like he'd thought. It was going to be Samantha.

And her *tio*.

J esus fucking fuck.

Fucking fucker fucking fuck.

Asshole monkey shit fuckers!

Bastian kicked the trash can over in his office, letting himself just lose his shit.

He hadn't asked for this—none of it. Stephen had been ten years older than him, had disappeared into the East Coast while he was a teenager, marrying Elizabeth and just becoming... sort of a mythical, former big brother.

He'd sent those babies gifts for Christmas, for birthdays. He'd gotten pictures of the kids, but—

"Why the fuck did y'all have to die?" He sat down, hard, trying to breathe, sucking air as the world just spun.

The accident was the beginning of the end of his uncomplicated, quiet life. He was allowed to be angry about that, wasn't he? It didn't mean he wasn't going to do what was right, but he didn't have to act like this was all okay every minute, did he?

And that little girl fucking hated him.

Hated him.

Bastian got it, and he was fighting not to snarl, but it had been a month, and she wasn't giving an inch.

And he knew Mama's heart was in the right place, but now he had this stranger in his house making him look like a fool. He'd been handling these kids for a month, and they were fine. He didn't need this know-it-all from up north walking in here like he knew better.

Even though Ash did probably know better, at least about the girl.

Weren't they supposed to like horses? A lot?

He had a foal now, he just needed to get her out there to see it.

Girls.

Mama said patience. He was trying.

There was a quiet knock on his door, interrupting his thoughts.

"Coming." He took a deep breath, stood, and forced his fingers to unfist. He opened the door with a smile.

Sort of.

"I cleaned up the kitchen, and your bathroom looks like a grown-up lives here again..." Ash gave him a crooked smile.

"Oh, wow. I—thank you." Fuck, how could he be mean now? No fair. No fair at all. "Are you a beer drinker?""

That smile grew wider, and Ash's blue eyes lit up. "I am a beer drinker."

"Excellent. Come on. There's a beer cooler on the back porch. We'll sit and chat some." He was embarrassed to admit that he didn't know a whole lot about this guy. Like nothing.

"Sounds great. I kind of showed up like Mary Poppins or something. I haven't even asked you what you really need yet." Ash followed him out of his study.

"I hear that. I'm not sure." And he wasn't sure about not being sure. He was a grown-up. He was supposed to be able to deal with this bullshit.

He was supposed to be a stud.

"Oh my god. This view. This is amazing. Beautiful." Ash took the Shiner he offered and stared out over his land. It was pretty spectacular if he did say so himself. "It just goes on forever."

"Thanks. Been in my family for generations." He knew every arroyo, every dip and nook. From the piñon to the sage brush, the cholla to the creosote, the reds and dusty greens of this chunk of high desert were sunk into his bones, and he—he couldn't imagine leaving it for anything. "What brings you to New Mexico?"

Asher laughed. "Really? You. Your family. Work, I guess. I was between jobs and told them I'd take anything anywhere, and the next thing I know I'm on a plane."

"From where?" Christ, Bastian couldn't imagine. He'd been on a few trips, seen a few places, but there had never been a time that he had thought he could just take a job anywhere.

"New Jersey. I worked for a family there that didn't need my services anymore. I'm still figuring out what's next for me. Ms. Stella... your mother told me this would be a temporary thing, until everyone is settled?"

"I guess, yeah." He wasn't sure how this worked. He wasn't sure how he ended up being a parent to these little kids who were damn near strangers.

Shit, that wasn't exactly the truth, was it? Elizabeth didn't have family to speak of, and Stephen and their folks had been... not estranged, but not fucking friendly for a long time. Way before Stephen had run off. So he'd been the only option.

Not fucking dying would have been the best option.

"My mom's afraid I'll let them all starve."

"Well, if you go by Samantha's review..." Ash grinned at him. "She's hurting pretty bad, huh? I'm so sorry for your loss, their loss. I don't really have words to... it's devastating."

"It is. The boys seem to be better, but they won't remember. Sammy just hates it here." But she was going to have to deal with that for another ten years, he guessed.

Ash sipped his beer. "She'd probably hate it anywhere right now. But I'm sure she had friends in Connecticut, and that's hard. It's not you, you know?"

"I know. She doesn't hardly know me to hate me. She'll figure it out." Or he'd send her to private school somewhere.

On the moon.

Where everything was super spicy.

"She will. That's partly what I'm here for, I guess, to help her figure this out. My job is to make your life easier, so you tell me what you need me to do."

How the fuck was he supposed to do that? Seriously? How did this even work? "So, how... what days do you want off and stuff? I'm not sure what all is involved."

Ash shrugged. "I'm mostly here to look after the kids, but I can cook, run errands, whatever. Free you up to do what you need to do. If I need time off, I'll let you know. Do you know what would be the most help?"

Keep me from losing my mind? "Sammy. She has to go to school and learn to be a normal kid. I don't know how to help her. I'm trying to get her into a therapist, but it's going to take months. *Months*."

"It's crazy, right? There aren't enough to go around these days and insurance... ugh. Okay. I'll spend some time with her. We need to get her interested in something. You're right, she's going to have to go to school soon, and I don't think she's your average kid. She's special. I'm not sure why, but she and I have an understanding already. Most kids aren't that sharp at what... eight, right?"

"I guess. I'm the baby, and I'm not an Einstein. I'm a cowboy." He thought the boys were easier—wild and nuts and into everything, but easier.

"Don't sell yourself short, you're great with them."

Right. He was great. He wanted to scream every second of every fucking day. Faboo. "Thanks, man. I appreciate it. I'm just trying to figure out how not to kill them and let them grow up and all." Surely that wasn't too much to ask.

"Seems like you're headed in the right direction." Ash drank his beer. "This is good stuff."

"It is." He sighed. "So, what do you need to know about the kids? What's important?"

"Oh, um. Well, practical stuff first, I guess. Allergies? Meds? Anything like that?" Ash relaxed in his chair and turned to look at him.

The idea of giving the twins medicine was nauseating. "No allergies. No meds. I mean, I give them baby Tylenol when they have a fever... does that count?"

"That's good to know. Hopefully, they don't have them too often. What do they like to do all day? Do you have a playroom? Do they like to be outside?"

"The boys run around. Samantha cries. I don't, but there is room. And God, I hope so because we're outdoorsy folks." They had seven bedrooms—his, three for the kids, two for the nanny suite, that left one upstairs, or they could make one downstairs.

"Hm. Okay. The boys need a playroom. You tell me where and I'll make it happen. Did all of their things come with them? Clothes, toys?"

He winced, because he had to. "They brought a few

things with them, and then the rest came, but Sammy freaked out, so I put it away for a few weeks until she felt better."

The whole thing had been a nightmare. Poor Sammy had been hysterical. Lost. He couldn't put her through that.

"Hm. Okay. That's… hard." Ash tilted his head curiously, eyes on him. "How are you? This is… a lot. On top of losing family."

"I'm just working, putting one foot in front of the other." And trying to understand what was what. Trying to have faith. Trying to figure shit out.

"So did you ask your mother to hire me?" That was a direct question.

"No. I didn't even know you were coming until yesterday. Mama came over last week during a massive meltdown." All three of them had been screaming and crying and throwing things.

"Wow. That has to be stressful." Ash chuckled. "I have to tell you, watching you run across your balcony chasing a naked little boy was a very interesting way to start my employment here."

"Yeah… I thought Will was going to throw himself off the damn balcony. Little ass." He laughed, though, because he did love them—all three.

"He's a live one. Curious and independent. His brother seems like an old soul, huh?" Ash was paying attention. Not that the boys made it difficult.

"Walt just needs a little time to breathe, you know? He loves the critters, loves to go outside and just play. Mama says he's just like me." Bastian didn't see it, but it didn't matter.

"He likes you." Ash nodded. "So your mom is close… and your dad?"

"They live in Chama. About two hours away. They have a bed-and-breakfast and all, but they drive out once a week."

"That's good. It's good for the kids to have that relationship. Especially for Samantha."

He nodded, but he didn't know if it was. Mama could have a little bit of a temper, and she was mourning her baby boy. Dad had way more the calm, easy energy that Sammy needed.

Ash shook his beer can. "Well, I'm empty. I think that's my cue to get a shower and get some rest. Tomorrow's my first day of work, right? I have a feeling I have a lot to learn."

"Let me show you where your rooms are. You've got the suite on the other side of the house from me." He smiled and opened the door.

"A suite? That sounds fancy." Ash followed him back inside. "How do the kids sleep?"

"The twins sleep like rocks. Sammy cries a lot." That was the only time he felt useful with her.

That was when she needed someone right there.

"Sounds like Sammy cries all the time. I'm so sad for her. I hope I can distract her."

"I hope so. I just want her to be okay. I just want her to breathe." And to not hate him.

"She will." Ash laid a comforting hand on his shoulder for a moment. "She has people who love her. She'll see that in time."

"Yeah, I hope so." He grabbed Ash's suitcase from the bottom of the stairs. "We have a housekeeper—Anna. She'll be here at six a.m. to make breakfast."

They headed up the stairs, and then, at the end of the hall was the red room. There was a sitting room with a television, a bedroom, and an en suite.

"Oh yeah? I wondered when you said it was her kitchen.

That's good to know, I'll make sure to make friends. Oh... wow. This is my room? It's enormous." Ash literally spun around like Maria in *The Sound of Music*. "I feel like a king."

"Both of these and the bath. Of course you can have free range in the kitchen. If you need another television, whathaveyou, holler. The Wi-Fi password is on the desk."

"Another television?" Ash laughed. "I think I'm good. This is... amazing. Thank you. I'll see you at six. Bright and early. Like, wow, early."

"No. No, the kids won't be up until seven-ish, and Anna can watch them if I'm dealing with things until you're up." He was up with the sun. Every fucking day.

These days he just didn't sleep.

"Oh, I'll be up. I might still be in my pjs, but I'll be up. Thanks again." Ash gave him a tired smile and ran fingers through wavy blond hair. "I'll keep an ear out for Samantha and the boys. You should try to get some sleep."

"Rest well. You have my cell if you need me." He smiled and left Ash to his business. Wylie would be coming with tacos in an hour or so, and they'd drink and talk until they didn't have anything else to say.

It was the way his life was, right now.

Maybe for a while.

Maybe forever.

3

Don't worry, I'll be up. Six o'clock is fine. Totally fine.

Six o'clock was not fine. It was fucking early, and he was not a fucking early person anymore.

He was once, when he was younger and would work with kids who also got up early, but Casey and Caroline were teenagers now, and they didn't get out of bed until they had to.

He'd gotten used to sleeping until eight or nine.

But he said he'd be up, and so he was, stumbling around brushing his teeth and pulling clothes out of his suitcase.

Ash probably should unpack today. He was going to do it last night, but it was so much room to figure out and the bed was enormous and calling to him, and he just... got in it.

He found jeans and a T-shirt, pulled on his sneakers and fixed his hair, as much as it would fix, before taking a breath, finding a pre-coffee smile, and heading downstairs.

"Anna! Anna! Anna!" The singsong was absolutely Will, so loud, so happy.

"Que pasa, Guillermo?"

"His name is Will." And there was Samantha.

Oh boy.

"Buenos dias," he said as he walked into the kitchen. Then turned to Samantha. "Bonjour."

Coffee. He needed coffee.

"Buenos días! Mucho gusto. Te gustaría un café?" Anna, who was as tiny as her husband was huge, was already at the coffeepot, pouring out.

Samantha almost smiled at him. Almost. "Bonjour."

Almost was a step in the right direction.

"Yes, please. How do I say that in Spanish?" He grew up in Jersey and worked in Manhattan. He knew a few words, enough to be polite, but he didn't speak Spanish. "Café" was obvious enough, though.

She beamed at him, winked and handed over the coffee. "Te dices, *si, por favor*. It's nice to meet you. I'm Anna."

"Si, por favor," he repeated. "I'm Ash. It's very nice to meet you." He took the coffee and took a sip. It was dark and rich and perfect. "Mmm. Bueno. Thank you."

"So, you'll have to tell me all the things you crave. We have enchiladas planned for tonight."

Samantha groaned, but Anna simply ignored her.

"That sounds amazing. I'm up for trying anything new, I've never been here before so it's all new to me." He sat with Samantha and gave her knee a pat. "So, do you usually cook? Do you need me to do anything to help?"

"I make four suppers a week, and then I make sure there are things to throw in the fridge. Señor Bastian works so hard, you know?"

"He seems very busy, yes. He has a lot on his plate right now. I'm here to make his life easier too." He gave her a smile. "I met Wylie for a minute yesterday."

"I'm sorry." Her laugh rang out, so merry, and the boys

cracked up. "He's a great husband, and he adores the boss. They've known each other for eons."

"Seems like it. Whoo, he smelled bad yesterday." He laughed. "Great smile though. We're supposed to have a beer soon, and he said he'd introduce me around." He sipped his coffee again, stomach starting to growl.

"Absolutely. They'll all be in for breakfast soon. I was thinking French toast sticks, syrup, and bacon."

That made the kid in him happy. "Ooh. Sounds good." He looked at Samantha. "French toast sticks sound pretty good, right?"

She frowned, then shrugged and nodded. "Yes. Thank you, Anna."

"I promised you yesterday I'd make your choice today."

Will frowned. "Hafta potty."

"Oh, I got you, Will." He lifted Will out of his seat and picked Walt up too. If one had to go, the other would be two minutes behind. "Where are we going?"

"There's a powder room down the hall and a full bath off the laundry room." She pointed to a huge laundry with commercial washers and dryers, folding tables, sinks and a door to a bathroom.

"Whoa." He couldn't wait to do laundry. "Okay boys... go, go, go." He herded Will toward the full bath because it was closer. "Oh, you boys need a stool in here." He set Walt down, helped Will wiggle his pants down, and sat the boy on the potty. "All good? Push that little man down, bud."

"Uh-huh. Sing the Pee Pee Song."

Walt started singing, "Gotta potty! Pee pee, pee pee pee, pee pee pee pee!"

Then Will started singing along.

He was not going to laugh. Nope. No laughing. He did try to sing along, though. "Pee pee!" When Will was done, he put Walt in his place and helped Will get dressed again. "Good work, man."

"Sank you! Sing for Walt now."

They started singing, but Walt was mouthing the words already, concentrating hard.

It had been a while since he had kids this little to look after, he'd forgotten how fun they were. Even if they were also challenging.

Walt had bigger things going on. "Do you have a poop song too?"

"Uh-huh." Will wiggled. "Pooping is great! Pooping is good! Pooping is stinky 'cause it used to be food! Go-o-o-o-o poop!"

He laughed that time, but somewhere in the back of his head he was thinking about their mother, who'd loved them enough to sing silly poop songs with the boys. He could totally carry on the tradition for her.

Walt finished and they all got cleaned up and washed up, then headed back into the kitchen where Bastian and Wylie and a couple of other cowboys filled the room, pouring coffee, making noise, and getting in Anna's way.

He sat the boys in their seats again. He wanted to meet everyone, but he had a job to do too. He crouched next to Samantha. "You good? You want some more juice or anything?"

"I'm okay. Can I have my own syrup to dip in?"

That didn't seem like an unreasonable request.

"Sure, you can." He gave her a wink. "Let me go make that happen for you." He stood up and went to see if he could help Anna, putting dishes together for the kids and making sure Samantha had her own little dish of syrup. The boys could share.

The guys were loud and big and taking up a lot of room in the kitchen, but it was a friendly group.

"French toast sticks, huh?" Bastian said. "I love those."

"You just love to eat, Boss," one of the cowboy's teased, and Bastian nodded.

"You know it." Bastian put milk and juice on the counter before kissing Anna's cheek. "Smells great, lady. Thank you."

Ash laid low and stayed out of the way, listening and observing, giving the kids their plates and sitting with them to eat. "Look at this pretty little bowl I found for your syrup." He set the little painted ramekin full of syrup down for Samantha.

"Thank you." Oh, that was a smile. An actual smile.

Bastian was nonstop busy—giving direction, making another pot of coffee, answering a constantly ringing phone, scribbling notes. It was utter chaos.

Anna seemed to take it all in stride, serving up French toast, picking up plates, and putting them in the sink as guys finished eating, chasing Wylie away from the refrigerator.

"Is it always like this in the morning? All these people?" Samantha was his best source of information so far.

Samantha nodded. "They all talk and the phone rings and rings, and then they go outside, and it's hot."

"It's the southwest in the summer. Hot is kind of how it is, you know? They all have jobs to do to take care of this place, I guess." He took a bite of a French toast stick, humming at the warm syrup and rich eggy bread. "Oh. Yum. Good choice."

"They're yummy."

Bastian came over and sat as the cowboys trooped out. "Mornin', y'all. How are you?"

"Walt pooped!" Will cheered. "Yay!"

"Go, Walt!" Bastian cheered along, toasting with his coffee cup.

Walt's smile was huge, and he was going to be a blusher. So adorable.

"I learned some catchy songs this morning in the bathroom." Bastian was definitely busy, but Ash loved how he took a minute to sit anyway. He looked great too, rugged and outdoorsy and smelled like aftershave. "I learned to say 'yes, please' in Spanish too."

"Bueno. Los niños necesitan entiendo español, sí?" Bastian let Will feed him a bite of syrupy, sticky food. "It's important here to learn Spanish. It will open up so many doors."

"Yeah, for sure. The boys are young enough they'll just absorb it. Samantha and I are going to have to learn together." He was only here a few months; he wasn't sure how much he could really learn in that amount of time, but Samantha needed to get started. He was going to have to convince her somehow.

"The kids' dad, he was fluent in Spanish, but I don't know how much he kept up with it."

Didn't seem like much, given Samantha kind of defiantly didn't know any and clung to her French. "It'll just happen now that they're here." Bastian looked even more tired when he talked about his brother.

"Yes. I hope so. There's a class in Sammy's school. She'll love it, I hope. It's a good private school. Excellent academics."

"Nice." He looked over at Samantha who was staring down at her food while she ate, acting like she was ignoring them. "I think a chance to start a new adventure is kind of exciting. I've never been to a place like this. I'm sure I have a lot to learn."

"It's a great place to live, to grow up." Bastian glanced at Sammy, rubbed his forehead. "What are y'all's plans today?"

"I go working wif Tio." Walt sounded very sure.

"Well, I think we'll take a nice walk and see what everyone is doing, and then maybe if it gets hot, these guys can watch a movie while I figure out what they need for their playroom? I might ask Samantha to help me with that." She still wasn't looking up from her breakfast, but she was eating so he let her be.

Will glanced from Walt to him to Bastian. Then he babbled at Walt who shook his head.

"No. Wif Tio."

So, Walt was a little bit of a three-year-old troublemaker. "We'll make sure to see Tio, okay? But he's got a lot of work to do, and we need to let him do it."

Walt stared at Bastian, the expression heartbroken, and Bastian smiled at him. "I tell you what; you be good for Mr. Ash this morning, and this afternoon after lunch and naps, we'll go see the puppies and play in the sprinklers, okay?"

Walt frowned for a second, then smiled suddenly. "Puppies! Okay."

"I love puppies." He was about to ask what kind they were when Will chimed in too.

"Puppies!"

Ash nodded to Bastian. "Sounds like a plan. Thanks."

"Perfect. Tell Anna if you need anything. She does the ordering—food, supplies, whathaveyou. Just text or give her a list." Bastian kissed both the boys as he stood. "Y'all be good. Love you."

He'd better get Anna's cell number. "You bet." He shifted over so Bastian could get a better view of Samantha and bumped shoulders with her. "You'll come see the puppies with us, right?"

"I don't like dogs."

Bastian's lips tightened. "Then you can stay in your room and pout, honey. Totally up to you. I'm off. You don't run off, Walter James, okay? If you're good, we'll hang out this afternoon."

"Luff you."

"Oh, I love you all too. I'll be back for lunch. Tuna fish! Yay!"

Sammy sighed. "I hate—"

"Everything and everyone. We know. Trust me, we *all* know." Bastian grabbed his phone. "Holler if you need me, Anna. See you at noon."

Bastian left the kitchen, Anna sighed, and Sammy started crying.

Will and Walt glanced at each other, then they went to hide under the table.

He put a hand on Samantha's knee and sipped his coffee, letting the dust settle a little. He couldn't blame Bastian for being frustrated, and Samantha knew very well that she was being contrary.

"Let's all go get dressed, and then we'll take a walk and see the land a little bit, okay? I'm curious, I want to see what everyone does here." He stood and put a hand on Samantha's shoulder. "Anna, is it okay if I leave you the dishes? I'll help from now on, but..."

"No worries, Señor Ash. I've got it. I'll make a pack of water for you to take on your walk." She smiled gently. "That's a rule, around here. You always take water with you."

"Seems wise. I'll try to remember." Water. It was a desert after all. "Come on everyone... Will, Walt, come on, boys. Samantha, go on up and get dressed, please."

The boys came out and headed for the stairs, but Samantha was slower to move. "Samantha."

"He's so mean. Why didn't they leave me somewhere nice?" Her cheeks were red hot, burning.

He wasn't going dignify that. Bastian wasn't any meaner to her than she was to him, but she wasn't in a frame of mind to see that right now. "Come on upstairs. We can talk while we walk, okay?" He offered her his hand.

"Okay." She took his hand. "Are you here so someone likes me?"

"I do like you, but no. I'm here to look after you and your brothers so that your uncle can get some rest, work through how sad he is after losing his brother, and get back to work. He's very upset too." He kept hold of her hand as he followed the boys up the stairs.

"He didn't even know them. He just called and sent presents. Mommy said that. That we were a family, just us."

He nodded. "You were a family. But just because your dad didn't want to spend time with your uncle doesn't mean your uncle didn't love him or miss him. Sending presents means he loves you and wanted to know you too. Your mom and dad didn't have control over how your uncle feels, you know?"

He put that out there, even though it was a lot for a kid to work through, because he felt like Samantha might at least think about it for a while.

"I just miss them and my friends and my house. My mom was really nice, and no one here liked her."

"Of course you miss them. You loved them. It doesn't matter how anyone else felt about them at all. They were your parents, and they loved you too. Plus, Connecticut was your whole life, right? This place is different. Different isn't bad, but it's a lot. *A lot.* And you're just one small person." The boys ran into their rooms. "I'm from New Jersey. I get it. I don't know anything about anything here."

"I've been to New Jersey. This place is way bigger than Connecticut. *Way*."

"Way," he agreed. "I think maybe this *house* is bigger than Connecticut." He winked at her.

She actually giggled. "Right? For just one man! Crazy!"

He looked at her with wide eyes. "Totally crazy." Then he laughed and gave her a little push toward her room. "Get dressed. We have so much to talk about."

She smiled, an actual smile, and disappeared into her room.

Something went crash in Will's room, and Ash hurried in that direction.

Score one for the new nanny. Time to wrangle the twins into clothes before they set the house on fire.

4

Bastian managed to calm himself down and start back to the house for lunch in a fairly good mood.

MOM

How's the new guy?

His mother had the worst timing.

BASTIAN

Fine. Gentle. Not used to being at a ranch.
Sam likes him.

That, at least, was a great idea. Bring in someone that was from the same area as Sammy had grown up.

MOM

Thank God. I worry about you.

"Then why the hell aren't you here raising these kids? Why are you hours away?" he muttered.

BASTIAN

I'm fine. Going in for lunch. ttyl.

Okay. Good mood. You have to spend time with the twins. They deserve your smile. You can do this!

He opened the kitchen door and called out. "Hey, y'all! I'm home."

"Tio!" He heard a stampede coming from the den and two little boys appeared and practically leapt into his arms.

"You got them?" Ash called from somewhere. "We'll be there in a minute."

"I do! Hello, mis sobrinitos. Cómo están? Bien, sí?"

"Yes! So good. We played." Will kissed his cheek and wiggled to get down, and Walt just stayed, holding on tight.

He started getting lunch together while the boys babbled about running outside and playing with toys that Ash found in a box. Ash and Samantha joined them a few minutes later. Samantha's hair was pulled up in a ponytail, a bandana holding her bangs off her face, and she was flushed like she'd been working.

Ash was smiling and a little sweaty, and he had a gray smudge on one temple. "Hey, there. Busy morning?"

"It was. What all have y'all been up to?" Lord have mercy, that was cute as all get out.

"We took a long walk, the boys ran around, and Samantha and I climbed a weird tree. Then we came back and had a ton of water, and the boys have been watching a movie while Samantha and I have been moving furniture and carrying toys around to that downstairs room you offered as a playroom. She's got some great ideas. We're going to need a few things."

"Good deal. Just make a list, and we'll get it taken care of." He wasn't sure if he was supposed to be excited or act blase.

"Can I help?" Ash stepped up right beside him. "Are we doing sandwiches or...?"

"The boys just throw the bread on the floor, so I do crackers. There is bread, though..." He glanced at Sammy. "You want bread or crackers?"

Sammy met his eyes, and he was ready for a fight. She pursed her lips. "Bread," she said as if it were painful. She didn't say she didn't like it this time though.

Ash nodded. "Bread for me too, I think. Do you keep it in a drawer...?" Ash opened and closed a couple of drawers.

"There's a bread box right here—" He opened the box, the scent heavenly. The tortillas, bagels, English muffins, and bread lived in there.

"Oh. That's nice." Ash pulled out a loaf. "The boys told me all about the puppies on our walk. They can't remember names, though. Do you keep them? Give them away?"

"They don't have names yet. We'll keep one of the boys to stud out, for sure, and then all but two are asked for. They're registered Great Pyrenees, so they sell for around fifteen a piece." He loved his pack—his big stud was Boudin, and the three bitches were Blossom, Bubbles, and Buttercup.

"Fifteen... hundred?" Ash stared at him. "For a dog?"

"Yes, sir. Per puppy. They're a solid lineage." And they bred smart and big.

"Wow. I can't wait to see them. I don't think I've ever seen a dog worth that much money." Ash made three sandwiches and put them on plates. "Do you want lettuce or tomato or anything? Samantha? How about you?"

"Oh, please. There should be anything you need in the fridge." There was always a plate of veg.

"Lettuce...please?" Samantha answered quietly.

"You got it." Ash got the plate out and fixed up their sandwiches, then took Samantha's over to her. "I am hungry. We've worked up an appetite. And those boys are no joke."

"Oh, I don't know—I think they're funny as all get-out." He winked over, trying to keep it light and easy. "So tell me, what all are y'all planning for the playroom?"

Ash looked at Samantha. "Well, we want to paint the room a light blue, add a couple of low bookshelves and some bins for toys, and we were thinking a couple of beanbag chairs... Was there anything else?"

She nodded, not quite meeting Bastian's eyes. "Table and chairs for art and a Lego table too."

"Sounds great. I love that idea. Maybe a washable rug for under the tables. Those floors will get cold in the winter." And the hardwood floors weren't the most forgiving on earth.

"Yep. Great idea. How do we do this? Do we run to the store?" Ash sat between the boys and Samantha, leaving the spot across the table open for him, and helped Walt with his crackers.

"If you want, or you can make an order online and have it delivered. That'll save you a few hours of driving around." He pondered that. "The paint we can probably grab in person or have one of the hands stop for it."

"Great. I thought the two of you could paint it, knock it out fast while I wrangle the boys." Ash gave him a wink.

Oh, little fucker. Still, he didn't mind. If Sammy was willing, he was. He liked painting okay. "Sure. I'm in. Sammy?"

Sammy shot Ash a whole dissertation's worth of side eye, but she glanced at him and nodded. "I am in too. I'm good at painting."

"Cool." Huh. "Did you know what color you wanted exactly, or did you need to look at paint chips?"

"Paint chips?" Samantha's expression turned curious. "What are those?"

"You know when you go to a hardware store, and they have all the different paint colors all over on pieces of paper? Those are paint chips." Look at him, having a conversation with his niece.

"Well, maybe we should get some chips, then. There's a lot of blues... light blue and navy and cobalt and cer...uh... cerleo...something."

"Cerulean! I love that word. Sure. You want to drive out to the hardware store? We can." They could even grab an ice cream on the way home.

She glanced over at Ash again, and Ash nodded to her. Then she looked back at him, took a breath and said, "Okay."

"Cool. After lunch?" Jesus. Breathe. Okay. No panicking. He was not going to fuck this sideways.

Hopefully.

Samantha nodded, sitting up straighter in her chair. "I'm free after lunch."

"This is good tuna fish. I like the flavor." Ash took another bite and helped Will with a cracker, even though Will clearly didn't think he needed help.

Walt frowned. "Go bye-bye too?"

Oh, shit. He'd promised the boys he'd play in the sprinklers. Dammit. "I thought I'd pick up a swimming pool at the hardware store and bring it back for you to play in."

"That is a great idea. A pool, Walt!" Ash did his best to sound very excited. "While they're gone, we can find your bathing suits and maybe go outside again and run."

Walt chewed on his cracker, thinking hard. "Puppies?"

"Yes. Puppies after I get back." This boy was a negotiator.

"So how was your morning?" Ash asked him, and he actually sounded interested.

"Busy. Worming day, and I had to broker a deal for a couple of horses I wanted."

"Worming. Like worms? Like fishing worms?"

He was pretty sure Ash was completely serious.

"Like worming livestock as in getting rid of." Bastian winked at Ash. It wasn't pleasant, but a critter dying from infestation was worse.

Ash looked horrified. "Oh. Ew. That sounds... wow."

"Yup. So. Much. Fun." He waggled his eyebrows and took a big bite of his sandwich.

"I hope you washed your hands..." Ash grinned at him, then took a big bite of his too.

"Always. *Always* wash your hands in this line of work."

Ash laughed, the sound easy and happy. "Point taken."

"Go on horses?" Walt asked, and he shook his head.

That boy was going to be sneaking out to the stables in no time. "No, sobrinito. We'll take the truck. It's too far for the horses, and we'll bring back too much stuff."

"Can you imagine Tio trying to bring back a pool on a horse?" Ash gave Walt a wide-eyed look, and Walt giggled and threw his hands in the air sending crackers flying.

Will followed suit, and both boys laughed hysterically, and Bastian had to grin. Silly boys. They were lucky, because they didn't remember much. They didn't have as much to miss.

Sammy had memories.

There was nothing for it, though. He just held her through nightmares at night, let her hate him in the day, and held onto his temper. It was the only answer.

He didn't understand why Stephen and Elizabeth had to die. It was a stupid accident. A rock hauler had a brake failure. No one was to blame—not in that way that he could feel all self-righteous. It had been an act of God.

Now he had three kids.

Praise Jesus and pass the tequila.

5

Ash was going to fucking die.

The boys were down for naps after twin colossal meltdowns, which they needed even more than he did. Bastian was right, they were funny most of the time. They were so different, and they cared about each other in adorable ways, but when they hit the wall, they hit it hard.

He flopped on the couch in the den, kicked off his shoes, and put his feet up on the coffee table, then pulled out his phone and texted Max.

ASH

> Great kids. So tired. There are a lot of animals I know nothing about on this ranch. There are puppies too. I thought I knew dogs… I do not know Great Pyrenees. Holy crap. Is it hot there? It's hot here. Like HOT.

Max was two hours ahead, which still confused him, and he had no idea if he'd get an answer.

So he tried a hook.

ASH

The dad is hot too.

Sure enough, he got—

MAX

OOOOO! TELL! Big Gay Daddy?

ASH

Doubtful. He's a cowboy. But he's big in a
cowboy way—shoulders, arms. He's got
these amazing dark eyes, the kind where
you can't see his pupils. So pretty. And he's
good with the kids.

MAX

Yeah? Are they nice? Have you ridden a
horse yet?

Horses? Hell no.

ASH

Yeah, not gonna ride a horse, thanks. The
kids are great. Food is different but good.
I'm learning some random Spanish.

MAX

Mas cervezas por favor?

Shithead.

ASH

No, like Tio. And lots of little pet names for
the kids that Bastian uses. I had a Shiner
Bock though. It was pretty good.

He liked beer. It could have been mediocre, and he still
would have finished it.

MAX

So, how long's your contract? Do you have
a decent room this time? Did I tell you I'm
going out with Alex tonite?

ASH

It's three months right now. My room is
AMAZING. Hang on.

He added some pictures to his text and sent them.

MAX

It's a suite! And I have my own bathroom
and this giant bed and a view of mountains.
CRAZY!

Alex... which Alex?

ASH

The tall Alex?

MAX

The tall hung Alex! Eeee!

Max sent him a dick pic, and yeah, impressive.

"Damn." No, he was not going to let himself be jealous
of a dick pic. That was ridiculous.

Ri-dick-ulous. He rolled his eyes and laughed at
himself.

ASH

Congratulations. I'm jealous.

MAX

Right? I promise to kiss and tell.

A blow by blow?

ASH

Once again, you're having orgasms, and I'm
not because I'm surrounded by children.

In New York, this wasn't a problem. He knew where to go on his days off. He could even walk out the door after the kids went to bed and meet people.

Here?

Cows.

Horses.

Puppies, chickens, and manure.

And fucking *cowboys*, which was so unfair.

He probably should have thought this through more fully before he marooned himself in the mountains among the straightest straight men in the whole damn country.

ASH

Have an orgasm for me, man.

MAX

I'm shooting for three.

Ha ha ha.

He shook his head, but it was what it was, and these kids did need him. Bastian was, at best, busy. At worst, he was a grouch and desperately out of his league.

And he wanted to know backstory. What the hell had happened? All Sammy said was that her parents died. No elaboration. Bastian's mom hadn't given him any details either, apart from there was an accident.

He wasn't sure he dared ask Bastian, because the guy was obviously so broken up. Was it even his business?

It was important to the children, wasn't it? To Sammy, for sure.

He looked at his phone, then quickly texted Bastian before he lost his nerve.

ASH

Interested in an adult dinner tonight?

Those three dots seemed to blink forever, then the text came in.

BASTIAN

Sure. You want to go out to Abuelita's? I can get Anna to watch the hooligans.

Oh. Look at that. He was thinking beers and a late dinner on the porch, but Bastian wanted to go *out*-out.

ASH

I know nothing and am happy to go anywhere.

BASTIAN

K. 7 work? Gets us home by bedtime 4 littles

ASH

works for me

He could understand Bastian not wanting to miss bedtime. He'd learned, quickly, that Sammy had terrible nightmares, and that every time, Bastian was right there, rocking her, holding her, calming her down.

Who would have guessed by the way they fought during the daytime? Poor kid needed to talk to someone, but it was even harder to find a therapist out here than in New York. In the meantime, he was doing what he could during the day, and Bastian seemed to have Samantha at night.

He should do something other than sit here on the

couch, shouldn't he? Take a walk or clean something or... sneak another one of Anna's chocolate chip cookies. Man, they were good, and Anna knew he liked them now, so his waistline was in big trouble.

In fact, the food at this house was amazing—Mexican food, barbecue, burgers. It was like living in a restaurant.

He hauled his butt up off the couch and headed for the kitchen. He'd get a coffee and a cookie and then see what was next. He hooked the baby monitor from the boys' room on his belt. He only carried the one from Walt's room, since Will always ended up in there anyway. For naps, he usually just tucked them in together.

Samantha was sitting at the kitchen counter, painting and singing with the radio. Anna was making tortillas and sang along.

"Hola! Buenas tardes, Anna." He wandered over to the coffeepot. "Bonjour, Samantha."

"Bonjour! Comment ça va?" She smiled over. "I'm painting a picture for the playroom."

"Hola, Señor Ash. ¿Qué tal?" Anna lifted the coffeepot in a clear offer.

That thing was always full.

He pulled down a mug and held it out for her to pour. "Uh... I don't know what that means." He laughed. "Thank you so much." He looked over at Samantha and rested the back of his hand against his forehead. "Je suis *fatigué*. Like whoa." All these languages were going to break his brain. He didn't even know that much French, and it was going to show soon.

"Que tal means how are you?" Samantha told him. "You answer, bien, gracias."

Okay, then.

He looked at Anna, and winked, grinning. "Bien,

gracias." He took his mug and went to the table where Samantha was sitting. "Can I see? The playroom is coming along great, but it does really need art."

"It's an axolotl. It's my favorite animal."

"Are salamanders animals?" It was an adorable painting, and Samantha was quite the artist. She was also quite the student, it seemed. How many eight-year-olds even knew what an axolotl was? He only knew because one of the teenagers had done some kind of report for school on it. Weird swimming salamander thing. "That's going to be beautiful when it's finished."

"Thank you." She shrugged. "I told Uncle Sebastian about them. He said he would see if he could get me one, but there's a lot of paperwork, and it will take a lot of time."

"Well, nothing worth doing is easy, right?" He glanced over at the cookies on the counter, trying to convince himself he didn't need one. "Do you prefer Samantha? Sam? Sammy? Mantha? Nth?" He teased her, but it was an important question.

"I like Sammy, but not at school. That's not for the teachers. Just family." That was definite.

And interesting.

"Okay, that's fair. Samantha at school, then?"

"Uh-huh. Sammy at home is okay, though." She gave him a half grin.

"Sammy it is. You want a cookie? I need a cookie." He got up and reached for the plate.

"Can I have milk with it? I only have cookies with milk."

"Cookies are made for milk. If you're not having coffee." He went to the fridge and looked around. "Whole? Skim? Two percent?"

She was panicked, he could see it in the tightening of her face. "Normal milk. Like you drink."

"Oh, normal. Yep. I got it." He grabbed the two percent, figuring it covered the bases, and poured her a glass. "You want it over there, or do you want to take a break so you don't spill on your painting?"

She pondered for a second, then nodded. "I think I will take a break. I like my painting."

"Wise." He nodded and set her milk on the counter with the cookies. "So, Sammy. I've been wanting to ask you something, but I know you have strong feelings, and I don't want to make you mad or anything. I'm just asking as a friend. We're friends, right?"

"I guess so. I mean, I'm not going to do anything wrong just because you ask me to, though. So don't ask."

He forced himself not to grin at her. "Oh, never," he said seriously. "I just have a question. I want to understand what's up with the whole school thing."

She tilted her head. "What do you mean?"

"Well, you're a very smart girl. So, I know you understand that you can't go back to Connecticut."

She sighed. "I know. I want to, though. I miss my house and all my friends."

"That I totally understand. Moving is hard, and usually people move because they want to, not because they have to. Everything you're doing is hard. New is scary too. I was thinking you should go down to the school before school starts and maybe take a tour. With your uncle or me, whoever you want."

"Do you think they'll all hate me because I don't have a mom or dad?"

He felt his heart break a little bit. Kids were going to ask questions; that was natural, and Samantha—Sammy— would have to figure out how to answer them. "Would you hate someone that didn't have a mom or a dad? Of course you wouldn't. I only had a mom. I didn't even know my dad. My best friend Max was raised by his grandmother. I bet you'll meet people with all kinds of families."

"Yeah? But what do I say? I have an uncle? What about Girl Scouts? Moms take you to Girl Scouts."

"Well, nannies take people to Girl Scouts too." He winked at her.

"Do they? Do they have Girl Scouts here? Everything is different. I have to drive a long way to go to school. I used to walk when the weather was nice." She sighed dramatically.

"I am sure we can find you a Girl Scout troop. And driving to school is awesome. All that time to talk and listen to music? So much fun." Everything was definitely different, she was right. He felt way out of his element too, but work was work, and he had decided it would be an adventure. He'd just have to convince Sammy the same.

"Maybe. I don't know. I'm just tired." She shook her head. "I miss my mom."

He nodded. "I bet. Moms are important, and yours loved you very much. This is hard. You're not sleeping very well, huh?"

"Uncle Sebastian says it's okay."

"It's totally okay. And I'm glad you have him; he loves you. I just wondered if I could help."

"They are coming to get me, but they're all slimy and bloody and rotting and gross." Her eyes filled up with tears. "I love them, but they're all bitey..."

"Wow. That's... scary." Jesus. That was terrifying in fact. "Well... why do you think you're having those dreams?"

She wouldn't meet his gaze. "Because I wished for them to come back."

"Oh. Yeah. That makes sense." He really couldn't imagine the horror Sammy was living right now. Parents were just always there, so to have them suddenly not there... he didn't even know how a kid was supposed to process that. "Well, maybe they're still here in other ways already. I think that's just your brain playing not-nice games with you. You have plenty of good memories of them up in there, right?" He tapped the top of her head playfully.

"Not enough. Uncle Bastian says the dreams will stop. He promises they will, but what if he lies?"

He looked at her seriously, because lying wasn't something to play with. "Do you honestly think he would lie to you? After everything he's done and wants to do for you? Come on. I think he's right. And I think if you fight those nightmares with your favorite few memories, they will stop even faster."

"He is sort of bad at happy lies, huh?"

He had to grin at that. Sammy was such a kid in some ways and so far beyond her years in others. "Well, yeah. Maybe. But I don't think being bad at lying in general is a bad thing."

She rocked a little, chewing on her cookie meditatively. "I don't know. Daddy said that it was important in business. That Uncle Sebastian could have been famous-er and rich. But he's pretty rich..."

Famous? That he needed to know. "Famous for what?"

She blinked. "I don't know. He doesn't seem to be... I mean, he's just a cowboy, right? Like he's not a president or a movie star or a singer."

Just a very rich cowboy, and his money had to come from somewhere. "Well, he must be *something*." He leaned closer to her. "We'll have to figure it out."

"We could ask him. He's bad at lying."

God save him from literal children.

"True. We could. What would we say though? Hey, man, how come you're not famous-er?" He winked at Sammy.

"Hrmm... Uncle, have you ever thought about being president?"

"Say, are you secretly a movie star?"

She giggled softly. "Do you want to sing KPop?"

Oh, good one. "Have you ever had a modeling career?"

She wrinkled her nose. "Can you imagine? Uncle Bastian is *not* cute."

Cute? Maybe not to an eight-year-old girl, but Bastian was all cowboy. Handsome, dark-eyed, and just the right kind of rough around the edges.

What was going through his head when he took this job in Straightsville? He was rethinking his life choices.

"Well, he doesn't need to be cute. He has a big ol' hat." He laughed. "Are you all done?"

"He does to other cowboys! He needs a boyfriend."

"Probably a girlfriend, but yeah." Boyfriend. This girl was New England to the bone. "That would be nice for him, huh?"

She looked at him like he was insane. "He likes boys, Ash. He doesn't lie about stuff. I asked him why he didn't have a wife, and he said he was going to maybe have a husband someday, but right now, he was too busy."

"Oh." He tried to keep from staring at her. "Oh, well, great. Good for him. A shame he's so..." *Single.* "Busy."

Fuck a duck. He'd just moved in with the only gay cowboy in existence. Bastian was like... the Loch Ness Cowboy. Sasquatch in a wide-brimmed hat.

"Yeah. Can I finish my painting now?" And just like that, she was done with any discussion. Really, she'd done pretty well, he thought.

And that was okay; he was too. She'd just blown his

mind. "Yep. Yes. You paint. I should... I have to... do a... thing. In the den. Happy painting!" He squeezed her shoulder and fled the kitchen.

Dude. Bastian was gay?

Fuck, and he'd just asked the man to have dinner.

Or... wait. Had Bastian invited him out to dinner?

Oh, God.

He pulled out his phone and texted Max.

ASH

the cowboy is gay

He had to figure out what he was going to wear before the boys woke up.

6

"Tio! Tio! Tio! Tio!"

The boys were screaming for him, bouncing and laughing as he headed into the house.

"Hey, y'all!" He scooped up the boys for kisses and grubby-handed hugs. He had to change for supper anyway. "How are you? What did you do today?"

"Ran outside."

"Had apples for snack."

"And cheese."

"Yes! Cheese!"

"I took a nap in Walt's room, and I felled out of bed."

Walt giggled softly.

"Oh no! You fell out of bed?" He tickled them both. "Where's your sister?"

"Playin'," Will said.

"Puppies, Tio?" And there was Walt.

"He's been asking about the puppies for a half an hour." Ash had hung back as the boys ran to him but took a few steps closer now. "Will just kept saying 'soon, Walt, soon…'"

"All right. Sammy? You want to come visit the puppies

with the boys?" Bastian caught Ash's gaze. "You're welcome to come with."

Ash liked those little beasts.

Ash nodded and called again for Sammy, who appeared at the top of the stairs. "Puppies?"

"Okay." She came down slowly but walked right up to him.

"Have you ever thought about being president?" she asked.

Ash snorted a laugh.

"Me? No, ma'am. I wouldn't like that at all. I love my job as a cowboy and a rancher." Weird, but cute. "Do you want to be president some day?"

"No. Something way more interesting than the president."

"Puppies!" Walt got loose and ran for the door.

"Slow down, Walt!" Ash chased after him, but Bastian wasn't worried. Walt couldn't get past the safety lock on the front door.

He'd had to put those on every exterior door the very first day after the boys moved in.

He was safe for a couple of months, at least.

"What's more fun than president?" He propped Will more firmly on his hip and unlocked the door once he knew Ash had Mr. I Love Dogs More Than Life.

"An astronaut." That was said with absolute conviction.

"Yeah? That would rock. I love that idea." He wondered if he still had a telescope up in the attic...

"Is it okay if Ash takes me to Girl Scouts? He says that nannies do that too like moms do, so it wouldn't be weird."

"Of course it is. Girl Scouts rocks. Ash is here to help, right? And if he can't take you somewhere, then I will."

"A big cowboy at Girl Scouts?" Sammy laughed, but he

could tell it wasn't meant to be mean. "You and everybody's mom..."

"Yep. Me and everybody's mom. Moms like me." Most women did, as a rule.

"Cool. Ash said there has to be a troop, so we'll find one." This was a step in a whole new direction. Joining Girl Scouts meant that Sammy planned on staying, instead of asking when they were going back up to Connecticut.

"I'm sure there is. I'll find out where and when they meet. They have 4-H here too. You might like that." He'd been big in 4-H, and so had Stephen. "Your dad liked that."

"4-H?"

"Almost there, Walt." Ash was laughing as he shifted Walt to another hip, but he looked about ready to toss the boy over his shoulder.

"Yeah, it's like a group that meets and people do animal things and craft things and cooking things. It's run by volunteers, and it's all about learning things by doing them. I raised cattle in 4-H and showed them. Your dad did sheep."

"Is that what he thought you should be more famous for? Cattle?"

He didn't follow. "Well, if I'm known for anything, it's the cattle, but I'm not famous, honey."

His breeding stock might be, in super specific channels.

"Oh, okay." Sammy shrugged.

"Puppies!" Walt's one-track mind was hilarious. Maybe he'd be the 4-H guy.

Maybe. Shit, he'd have those two in 4-H as soon as humanly possible. The twins were genetically bound to this land.

He hoped Sammy would be too, but he wasn't sure. He'd have to wait and see.

Ash put Walt down as they went into the barn. "Careful, Walt. Slow down, buddy."

"Remember, they're babies. They can be scared." He smiled as Blossom came up to him, woofing softly before going to Sammy to beg a pet.

Buttercup and Bubbles were undoubtedly with Boudin working. The hands had them going through their paces daily, guarding the sheep, keeping the coyotes and mountain lions warned away.

The puppies were starting to be more and more active, and he was going to have to have one of the guys start socializing them.

Walt plopped down to play, and Will ran over to him. "I want that one," Will said with the authority only a three-year-old could muster.

Walt started pointing. "I want that one and that one and that one and that one."

"There are plenty of puppies." Blossom had given him eight. That was a gracious plenty. "Y'all just love on them—gently."

The barn erupted in giggles.

"Are you keeping them?" Samantha asked seriously. "My friend Alicia's parents gave all their puppies away. She didn't get to keep even one of them."

"We're keeping two, probably. This will be Blossom's last litter. She's had three, so she's going to retire and become a granny dog."

"Can I sit and read with a granny dog?"

"Blossom would love that. She's wanting to be a house dog, you know?" The others sort of came and went as they pleased, but Blossom wanted to be a pet, to be adored and snuggled.

Sammy seemed pleased with that answer. "I don't need a puppy. I need Blossom. I can brush her and everything."

Okay. Okay, he could work with that. "That would work. She'll need a friend who can help her. She'll have the puppies in here for five more weeks, but then she'll be looking for a place to be."

Sammy nodded once. "We will be friends."

"He's licking me!"

"I think that one is a girl, bud."

Will stuck his arms up, and Ash picked him right up. "Had enough licking?"

"Too much." Will rolled his eyes dramatically.

Walt, on the other hand, was wallowing in puppies, giggling and happy as if he was a pup himself.

"So, what are you wearing to dinner tonight? Is it casual?" Ash shifted Will to the other hip to see him better.

Casual? They were going to eat enchiladas. "I'm pretty sure I only do casual, friend. Shirt and jeans."

"Perfect. I have those. What time did you want to head out?"

"Anna's coming to feed the ravening horde." He saw Sammy's lips tighten, and he fought his smile. "She said she was feeling like pizza tonight."

Will liked that idea. "Peeza."

Walt actually looked up from his puppies. "Peeza?"

Sammy sighed. "Well, if pizza works for the boys, it's fine with me."

"I appreciate that, Sammy. It's very nice of you." Such drama. He was going to kill her when she was a teenager.

"Okay, Walt, time to get moving." Ash put a hand out to help Walt up.

"No...Tio. Puppies, *pease*."

"Tooners!" Will insisted. They got half an hour of television a day. Apparently, this was important.

"Come on, Walt. The puppies will still be here tomorrow." Ash set Will down so he could fish Walt up with both hands, and he caught Will's hand.

"C'mon, y'all. Mr. Ash and I have to go take a ride, but we'll be home by bedtime." He needed to wash up and all, change shirts, but whatever Ash needed to chat on, it shouldn't take long.

Ash wrestled with Walt a little, but the boy never really put up a fight. He had a powerful pout, though, and he pulled it out every time they left the barn. "I love puppies."

"And those puppies love you, sobrinito. They think you're amazing."

Walt beamed and reached for him.

"Oh. Look who wants you." Ash took a couple of quick steps to get closer.

He scooped both boys up into his arms. "Lead the way to the house, Sammy. We're marching."

"Marching?" Sammy jumped in front of him and marched, knees high, arms swinging. "March... march... march."

Ash fell in line to bring up the rear. "Left! Left!"

"Left, right, left!" Okay, if this was the way to make it work, this was what he would do.

Sammy marched and sang, and the twins sang along, obviously enchanted. She was their big sister, after all.

"So much noise!" Anna teased as they marched right in through the kitchen door.

"Hola, Anna!" Ash called as he came through the door.

"We're marching!"

"Mars-ing!" the twins agreed.

"March out of your dirty boots before you leave mi

cocina, por favor!" Anna meant business, and Bastian chuckled as Ash immediately took off his shoes.

"Aye, tan mala! So mean," he teased her, using his jack to help pop first one boot off, then the other.

"I heard someone wanted... pizza?"

"Peeza!" The boys jumped up and down.

Sammy just nodded.

"I'm going to change." Ash rested a hand on his shoulder. "I'll meet you down here in like, ten?"

"Works for me. You okay, Anna? Can you handle the boys? Sammy can handle herself."

"Of course, we'll be fine. Go enjoy your dinner." Anna was getting the boys into their seats, and she waved him off.

He went up and gave himself a spit bath, making sure that his decent jeans were clean enough to wear. He knew his shirts were fine.

He got dressed, grabbed his keys and his wallet, and headed back downstairs.

Ash was waiting in jeans and a T-shirt that fit kind of tight. He hadn't noticed Ash had some muscle on him until now.

"Hey, I don't see any dust on those jeans." Ash's eyes lit up with a teasing smile.

"I own one pair. It's a miracle." He winked over, shook his head. "I'll drive. Come on."

He waved to the kids, the boys waving back.

"Research." Ash winked at Sammy, also gave the boys a wave, then followed him out the door. "This is kind of nice; I haven't left the house since I got here."

"You know you can totally use the Suburban anytime, right? You aren't a prisoner." Mostly.

"Maybe once the kids need to go places—school, Girl Scouts, whatever. Otherwise, my job is to be where they are.

But thank you." Ash climbed into the passenger side. "Also, I've never driven anything this big."

"No? You've got tons of room to practice out here. It's so much safer than on a city street."

"The roads are definitely bigger than up north. I did drive that little rental here, but they took that away the next day. I'll get some practice time in before Sammy starts school."

Bastian nodded. That was logical and reasonable—two words that he absolutely associated with Ash. "Sure. There's a set of keys for you on the board by the kitchen door."

"Great. Thanks." It was quiet for a moment, and then Ash spoke up again. "This was a nice idea, going out. I was thinking a late-night dinner after the kids went to bed, but this is neat. I like going out."

"You've been cooped up." And he hadn't even thought about it. "It's time to show you around a bit. Abuelita's is classic New Mexican, and there's a tiny grocery store attached to it." It had all the necessities—tortillas, green and red chile, pinto beans, beer, conchas, guava paste, piñon nuts, and paletas for the kids.

"Sounds neat. I really don't know anything about New Mexico. I'm just trying to roll with the punches."

"You're learning fast. Do you like it?"

"So far, yes. You can't beat the view and your house is just incredible. The kids are fantastic." Ash chuckled. "Oh, and the dad I work for is a great guy."

He snorted, but it hurt, deep inside. He wasn't Stephen for those kids. He couldn't be. "I'm not a dad. I'm nowhere near qualified for that. I'm just the uncle."

Ash shook his head. "You're an uncle by blood. You're functioning as a father. Especially for those boys. They won't know any other dad. They might call you Tio, but uncle probably won't be what it means to them."

That was presumptuous for someone who had only just met them all. Still, those boys didn't mention their parents at all.

It was an enormous amount of pressure.

Ash glanced over. "Sorry. You don't really need another dose of reality right now; you've probably had enough for a while. That's why I'm here, right?"

"No. No, you're here because I have to work, because I've never done this, and because Sammy hates me." He even knew why, but he was so tired of fighting.

"Oh, you know better, don't you? She hates that she can't have her parents back, and she's angry about that. She trusts you. If it's not love yet, it will be. You were doing just fine before I got here. What you need is sleep and balance. *That's* why I'm here."

"God, yes. I just want one night—all the way through." He ached for that, actually.

"I'm working with Sammy. I'm trying to give her the idea that she can combat the bad dreams with good memories. Even just one or two. Use them like a shield or a spell against the nightmares." Ash nodded thoughtfully, like he was thinking this through even as he spoke about it.

"Yeah. I talked to an online therapist, just because I was scared to death." He'd been damn near hysterical, even.

"She's coming around fast, you know. She told me about the nightmares, about what they are, about why she thinks she is having them. She was very honest with me, and even just a few days ago, she didn't want to talk at all. I wanted to tell her she could come to me at night so you could sleep, but I think what you two have is special. She should always feel like she can come to you. I won't be here forever."

"No? You mean you're not in love?" Bastian chuckled softly. He was beginning to think he was alone in all the world.

"Oh. They're all wonderful. I'm just being realistic. Your mother said three months, and I guess that can change, but I can't let them count on me if I'm leaving them too."

"Oh." Three months? That was... the holidays. Oh God. "Hopefully, I can convince you to stay longer."

Ash leaned toward him a little. "You won't have to try very hard. You have great kids."

"I do, and... this was unexpected. They were young and healthy. I was shocked." There was the understatement of the century.

Shocked.

"Do you mind... can I ask what happened? You don't have to tell me; you can tell me it's none of my business. I'll respect that."

"It was a car accident. Literally an accident. No one was drunk. No one was stupid. One accident, and they're both dead."

"Just out of the blue." Ash glanced over, then shook his head. "God, I'm sorry."

"Yeah. I mean, we weren't close. We hadn't been close in a long time. He was ten years older than me. He was a city dweller. His wife didn't love our family."

"I got that impression from something Sammy said. She also said her dad thought you could have been more famous and more rich. I thought that was interesting."

Oh, for fuck's sake. Stephen had always had delusions of grandeur. Like their lives weren't big and amazing enough. As if they weren't blessed beyond all reason. "He wanted me to be a sculptor. I make weird shit out of metal for the yard and all. It's a hobby."

He'd put it all away after the boys had cut themselves the second day here.

"Oh wow. You do? Do you have a studio? Where do you keep it?"

"It's all in the garage. I'll put it out when the boys get older, or I'll make myself up a sculpture garden or some such." He'd get around to it.

"You'll have to show me sometime. It sounds cool." Ash was looking out the windows in all directions, taking in the scenery as they approached the restaurant.

It seemed a little old and worn down, but it was clean inside, and the food was amazing.

He found a space and threw the truck in park. "You ready?"

"I am." Ash flashed him a smile that lit up his blue eyes and then hopped out of the truck.

Someone was hungry, which was good, because he was too, and those enchiladas smelled like heaven on earth.

"Look at this place." Ash looked around like it was the most interesting restaurant he'd ever been in. "It's so neat. And it smells so good. You'll have to tell me what I should order."

"I'm getting the enchiladas with Christmas, but I've never had anything bad here. The stuffed sopapillas rock..."

Ash squinted at him. "With Christmas what?"

"Lord help you, you poor man." He waved to Christiana and grabbed a table. "So the state question is, red or green? Christmas is both. I always choose Christmas."

Ash looked completely lost. "How does a state have a question? You just randomly ask people this question? Hey man, red or green? Red or green... what?"

"Chile, man. Chile. Red and green chile. Red's smoky,

green's fruity, they're both magical." Folks lived without chile?

"Red or green chile." Ash laughed at himself. "Okay. This is a New Mexico thing for sure. I will definitely be ordering Christmas. Ho ho ho."

"Attaboy." That was the way to dive in. He approved. "What's your favorite food?"

"You know, I'm not picky. But I really like a cheeseburger. Preferably with bacon."

"Bacon. Mmm." He had raised a lot of cheeseburgers in his life.

"Mhm. Bacon. Some cheddar cheese is good too, maybe a jalapeno cheddar? You could throw some pickles on there or sliced avocado... good stuff."

"They have an amazing green chile burger here too. Nice and spicy." And he loved it. For lunch.

"Next time. I'm having what you're having this time. When in Rome... or New Mexico... same premise."

"Absolutely. Although I could totally murder a pizza one day."

"Samantha told me that pizza is one of her favorite foods, if you're looking for brownie points."

"Ah. Well, she's getting that tonight, and she wrinkled her nose at it, so..." He rolled his eyes. He'd keep that in mind.

"She needs to feel like she is in control of something. Food is easy." Ash reached across the table and touched his hand. "She trusts you. She wants you to love her. I told her you do."

"Of course I do. She's my kin." Like he wouldn't love her. Bah.

"She's a smart kid, huh?"

"Brilliant. She's going to be great." She just hated him right now.

Ash smiled at their server who set down chips and salsa for them. "Hola."

"Oh!" Ellie's dark eyes glinted and danced as she drew out the word as long as she could. "You must be the new teacher at the ranch, huh? You like it?"

Oh, he wanted to hear the answer to that.

"I think it's the most beautiful place I've ever been," Ash said simply. "And everyone has been so kind and friendly. I'm not really a teacher though. I'm just here to help out with the kids."

Ellie glanced at him, and he shook his head. "He's a good teacher. He's helping Sammy and the boys so much."

It was weird to say 'nanny', really. That made him feel... stuck up.

Ash shrugged and went with it. "Thank you. So, I think we're both having the enchiladas. With *Christmas*." Ash looked so pleased with himself.

"Nice." Ellie grinned at him. "Good choice. Iced teas?"

Ash looked at him that time. "Iced tea?"

Bastian stared at him, utterly confused by the question. "Yeah. Please, Ellie. They got Coke too, if you'd rather."

"Nope, iced tea's fine. I was just making sure that was what you wanted." Ash turned to Ellie. "Thank you."

"Sure. I'll bring them in a hot minute."

Bastian put his cowboy hat, crown down, on the seat beside him.

"I am pretty hungry." Ash picked up a chip, scooped up some salsa with it and stuffed it in his mouth. A second later, his eyes went wide. "Mm." He picked up his water and sipped it. "Oh. Hot."

"You want me to ask for mild?" Surely they had some...

Ash waved him off and swallowed the salsa. "I'm braver than I look."

"Feel free to have a beer. It'll help the spice." He knew all about that. He took a bite himself, humming happily.

"So tell me why you're known for your cattle." Ash braved another bite of the salsa. A smaller one.

"Have you ever heard of wagyu beef?" He could talk about livestock for days. It was his job.

"Of course. That Japanese stuff?"

"So I raise breeding stock for ranchers to create a better marbled product. I sell semen, some cows, but I focus on a small, well-bred, well-researched herd with amazing genetic lines." It wasn't glamorous, but it was lucrative, and he knew that these weren't feed-lot cattle.

"Wow. That's interesting. It sounds like quite an investment." Ash leaned back in his chair, watching him. "Honestly, I never thought about where my beef comes from."

"No? Well, it's a huge industry, and I—I feel like it's important that we are good conservators of the land and the animal. We're blessed to have what we do; I intend to honor that." Did that sound stupid? Stuck up?

The look in Ash's eyes was full of wonder. "That's amazing. I love that. I've never heard anyone say anything like that before. I'd love to learn more about it."

"Sure. I mean, you would?" Dude. That was surprising and wonderful and cool. "I can teach you all about it. It's what keeps us in chiles and horses."

"I would. Honestly. Where else am I going to learn something like this? Not in Jersey."

"No, I guess not. It's a different world." At least he assumed so. "So do you know how to ride?"

"Bicycles, yes. But if you mean horses? I've never been on one. They're beautiful though. Big. But beautiful."

"Well, if you want to learn, I have a stable full of babies that would love exercise."

"Okay. I'll learn. I'd love to. Assuming I have time, I do have kids to keep an eye on." Ash winked at him.

"You do, but I'll have the boys out riding soon. They need to learn." He couldn't remember not knowing how.

Ash blinked at him. "Wow, this young? That's not dangerous?"

"Well, I'm not going to put them on the back and slap the horse's flank..." Probably.

"Ha!" Ash laughed. "Will would probably love it."

"And Walt will be going, 'Puppies! Big puppies!'"

"Right?" Ash leaned over in his chair, giggling. "That kid is obsessed."

"He's going to be my cowboy, for sure." He grinned and shook his head. "Will's going to ride the rodeo."

Ash shook his head. "Will is aptly named."

"Goodness yes." He chuckled and shook his head. "He's magical. They all are, in their own ways."

"I agree. Did I tell you I've convinced Sammy to go visit the school before school starts? Do you think you could make a call and set up a tour for her?"

"I can. I've got the tuition paid for, and they're eager to meet her." He hadn't gone to private school, but he thought it was important for Sammy.

"Great." Ash looked pleased. "School will be good for her. The distraction, friends..."

"I hope so." Hopefully, she wouldn't alienate every single classmate she had.

Ash leaned forward and looked at him, holding his gaze. "Has anyone told you that what you're going through, what you're doing for those kids is *hard*? Like, actually hard, not just hard for you?"

"What?" He felt a little like he'd missed something, part of a conversation. He also felt seen, which was unnerving.

"I think sometimes people just assume others will adapt. Like changing your entire life overnight isn't a big deal. But this is a big deal, and if no one has acknowledged that yet, I wanted to. It's hard, and you're doing a great job."

"I—" He was trying. God, he was trying. "I want to. I never expected this. Ever."

Ash nodded. "How could you? Had you planned on having kids of your own one day?"

"Me? No. No, I'm—" Christ, he was queer as a three-dollar bill and a cowboy to boot. He wasn't in the closet, but he wasn't going to be able to have babies. "It was never in the cards."

"I've always wanted kids. Someday, maybe."

"I bet we can find you a nice local girl, Ash. They make gorgeous babies."

Ash burst out laughing. "Yeah, okay. I bet we could find you one too. But you don't want one any more than I do."

"I—" Wait, what? Did that mean? It meant. It had to mean that Ash was— "Eee-a-la, I was trying to be all decent and not 'boy nannies are gay'."

Ash was still giggling. "Boy nannies *are* gay, Bastian. I was feeling like, why the heck did I strand myself in straight-cowboy-ville, and then Sammy clued me in."

"Ah." He stopped, tilted his head. "You asked Sammy if I was gay?"

"No!" Ash shook his head. "Oh my god, no. But we were talking about whether you should have a modeling career, and she said you needed a boyfriend, and I laughed and told her she meant girlfriend, and she made it very clear that you plan to have a husband one day." Ash was still grinning and chuckling.

He stalled again. He was going to have to get more sleep. "Modeling... career?"

Ash shrugged and blushed a little. "Yeah. We, uh... we were joking around about ways you could be more famous. It's a long story. She was laughing, so I went with it."

"Oh lord, I don't want fame. I love just being me on the ranch. Stephen was the fame seeker."

"It certainly sounds that way if you talk to Sammy. Sounds to me like being you on the ranch is pretty good."

"Yes. I mean... yes." He chuckled softly, then began to laugh. "I guess it's more common to be wanting to be somewhere else, but I'm busy and happy. I'm home. I've got my dogs, my horses. I wish the kids had their folks, but I love them. I just... one day, Will's going to jump off the balcony."

"Guess you better surround the house with mattresses or trampolines." Ash shook his head. "Possibly child-proof the thing. How did you manage?"

"I fell off once and jumped off twice." He'd survived.

Ash snorted. "Well, then you won't be surprised when Will decides he can fly. Maybe Walt will talk him out of it. If he's not busy with the girls in the barn."

"True, or if Sammy doesn't toss one..." That he could actually see.

"She will definitely give you a run for your money." The food arrived and Ash's eyes went wide. "Ooh."

Okay, that made his heart glad. "Right? It's like magic."

"It looks that way." Ash picked up his fork and took a bite, chewing for a second before humming at him. "Mm. Good."

"See? I told you. Magic. I can remember my fifth

birthday party was here, and I had a sopapilla with a candle in it."

"Damn. You really do have roots here. What a great place to raise the kids. All that tradition." Ash was eating well, so he was really enjoying his meal.

"What about where you're from? You got deep roots?"

"Oh. Well, I do, I guess, or did. I kind of ripped them out of the ground a while ago." Ash shrugged. "They're very conservative roots."

"Ah. New Mexico is... well, we've all got someone in our family that's not average. All of us." They tended to live and let live.

"You're above average." Ash gave him a nod and took another big bite of his dinner.

He was an outlier, but he'd take above average. "So, do you love it? Nanny-ing?"

"It's a job I understand." Ash looked thoughtful for a second. "I love kids. I like helping out. I like feeling... like I'm a small part of the family."

"Dude, you're like a big part, aren't you? You spend a ton of time with them."

"Well, I'm not really. I'm hired help. But my former employer made me feel that way. So far, I feel that way here too."

"Well, good thing for you, I'm not your employer. I'm just the guy that has custody." Mama was the hiring entity. Thank God.

Ash laughed. "Oh, good point! Custody of the nanny. Your mother is quite a personality."

"You have no idea. Mama is a fierce warrior who defends her family with all her soul." He shook his head. He loved her, but damn.

"She was very clear with me." Ash sat up straight and

imitated Mama on the phone. "He's a good boy, but he's in over his head, and he needs help with the children. Especially the girl; she's a tough one."

Oh, man—that was either awful or amazing. "That rocked! That was *her*!"

"She was very kind and very direct on the phone. I accepted the job because it was obvious how much she loves you and how hard this has been on everyone. I knew I could help."

"You are. The boys—I was scared I was going to lose them. Like literally—" He put his fingers to his eyes like binoculars. "—oh boys!"

Ash laughed. "Legit. Totally legit concern."

"I tell you what... I mean, you say the words nap or bath or... come here and they're like smoke." He scooped up another bite of salsa.

"Samantha taught me a trick." Ash leaned over the table like he was telling a secret. "Walt likes the freeze game."

He leaned in too, whispering soft. "What the fuck is the freeze game, and is it as cool as it sounds?"

"Ha! Oh. You need to learn this trick. I will school you in the ways of the freeze game. You say freeze, and everyone has to stay perfectly still except for you until you say unfreeze. Simple, yet effective."

"Oh man. I like this game already, and the adult is always the winner!"

"Every damn time. And he hasn't figured it out yet. Will hasn't clued him in either. Walt likes to win."

"Rock on." They shared another laugh and ended up just grinning at each other.

"Pretty soon you'll know all the tricks and you won't need me."

Every time Ash said that, it made him a little queasy.

"Yeah. In fifteen, sixteen years, if I don't get them killed, right?"

And every time he made a suggestion that he might need Ash longer than contracted for, Ash seemed a little uncomfortable too. "Probably a little sooner. Sammy will be in astronaut school by then."

"True." Okay. Right. Ash was here for three months, right? No reason to be a titty baby about it. "I'll get her out to the school to tour it. Was there anything else you need me to do that I'm not doing?"

Ash blinked at him for a second, but the look disappeared quickly. "Nope. That's all for now."

"Cool. You know you're welcome to let me know if you need me. I'm trying to learn, and I'll be more present. I was just trying to catch up on work."

"That's what you should do. You don't need to be more anything right now. Catch up. Get some sleep. I'm here to help you, really."

"I appreciate it. I didn't think I needed the help, but I do." He'd needed a ton just to get through day-to-day.

"I like being needed. This is going to work out just fine." Ash leaned back in his chair with a groan. "Especially if you keep feeding me like this."

"Good to know. Feeding you is doable, absolutely."

"Christmas for the win." Ash patted his tummy.

"You know it. Christmas all the way."

7

Why-oh-why was this gig only three months?

Bastian was as kind and funny as he was handsome, not that Ash should be thinking about his employer that way. Okay, technically the cowboy was the son of his employer, but somehow that sounded even worse.

The kids were great, Bastian seemed to see him as a friend, and all the things he could learn here sounded like so much fun.

But he would never have time for it all. Not in three months. He wanted to learn about the cattle. He wanted to learn how to ride a horse. He wanted to hang out with the only gay cowboy in the whole world because how cool was that? And maybe Bastian wasn't the only gay cowboy after all.

Will splashed him, and he blinked at the boy he was washing in the tub. Wow.

Earth to Asher. How about you not let the boys drown, man?

He could hear Sammy in her bedroom, singing with her music like a little bird. So sweet.

"Everybody out of the tub." He stood and hauled Walt

out and wrapped him up in a towel, then reached for Will. "Out you go, buddy."

Will frowned at him. "I play?"

"I know, baths are fun. We'll play more tomorrow, okay? It's bedtime now. Time for stories." He held his hands out for Will.

Will frowned deeper, but then Walt squealed. "Tio! Up!"

"Hey, buddy! You're nekkid!"

Ash scooped Will out of the tub while he was distracted and wrapped him in a towel too. "Fantastic timing, cowboy."

"Thanks, man! I brought supper. Did the kids eat?" Bastian tapped on Sammy's door. "Hey, girlfriend, you got plans tomorrow?"

"The boys ate and are almost ready for bed. Sammy opted to wait for you to eat dinner."

Sammy opened her door and squinted at Bastian. "Who would I have plans with tomorrow? I don't *know* anybody."

"Well, I was wondering if you'd like to run to Santa Fe and tour the school, maybe see this place I found that has art lessons."

"Art lessons?" Sammy stood a little straighter. "Yes. Let's do it."

Oh, good work, Bastian.

"Cool. If you want, we can go out in the mid-morning, have lunch out and all. You know, see what art supplies you need for that, maybe stop at the bookstore." Bastian was trying hard to be casual and easy, to make this easy for Sammy.

"There's a bookstore? Okay. Can we get chicken fingers for lunch?" Sammy went right along, and Ash was super proud of both of them.

"Yes, and yes. Sure. You can pick wherever you'd like."

Sammy actually almost grinned. "Cool. I like that— picking. Ten o'clock?"

"Ten works for me. There's pizza downstairs."

"Oh. Yes. I'm hungry, thank you." Sammy left her room and headed right down the stairs.

He glanced at Bastian, each of them still holding a wiggly three-year-old and nodded. "Nice."

"Thanks. I'm trying to learn by example. Come on, sobrinito. Let's find jammies."

The compliment felt... amazing.

The next twenty minutes were more challenging, and he finally decided that the two of them putting the boys down together was too much stimulation for three-year-olds, so he slipped out of the room as Bastian finally got Will settled.

He didn't go far, though. He wanted to leave Sammy to her pizza and her privacy, so he hung out in the hallway, playing around on his phone until Bastian snuck out of the bedroom.

"All good?"

"Walt's got his puppy stuffy, and Will has his blankie. All is well. Decent day?"

"Good day. You?" He was settling into a routine with the kids, and he liked it.

"Not bad. Got a new stallion in. Ready for a beer. You in?" Was that a flirty smile?

And if it was, should he have noticed? "I so am. I need to get Sammy in bed first." Sammy pretty much put herself to bed, but he liked to say goodnight.

"We can go have food with her. I hate to have her eat supper alone." Bastian clomped down the stairs, boots clacking away.

"Oh, right. Dinner." He'd been a little blinded by that smile. "Pizza."

"Nom nom nom." Bastian's laugh drew him down the steps. "Let's eat."

"Sammy! Did you eat all the pizza? We're coming," he called from the bottom of the steps.

"Yep. It's all gone. Every slice." She actually sounded cheery.

He ran into the kitchen as if in a panic, playing with her. "You ate all the pizza?"

She blinked innocently, then started to laugh, just cracking up. "Got you!"

"Oh my gosh." He put a hand over his chest. "You so did. I was thinking, how could that little girl put away so much pizza?"

"Pizza is yummy. I can eat three whole pieces sometimes." She pushed over the boxes. "One's got hot peppers on it."

"Green chile. I made sure to get one without any, though." Bastian handed him a plate.

"Well, I have to try that. Obviously." He held out the plate he'd just been given so Bastian could load on a slice.

The pizza was different than in New Jersey, but it didn't suck. It was a thick, sweet crust, and the green chile was spicy, but fruity.

"Did you try the chile, Sammy?" He sat with her and took another bite. "Spicy."

She wrinkled her nose. "No. I don't like spicy. I don't like it at all."

"Give it time. I didn't like spicy food when I was your age either, but now I'm more adventurous." He started to say that kids usually didn't like spicy food, but the boys didn't seem to mind it.

Bastian nodded like it was no big deal. He was obviously

learning not to respond, that Sammy was searching to upset him.

Parenting was sometimes nothing more than instinct and mind games.

"What are your after-dinner plans, kiddo? Reading? Bath? Movie before bed?"

"I'm going to watch the Troll movie and play with my Barbies." She picked cheese off her pizza. "What about you?"

"I'm going to sit on the back porch, watch the sun set, and drink a beer with your uncle."

"Beer is nasty."

"I remember thinking that too," Bastian admitted.

"I... really don't." Ash laughed. "I only ever remember liking beer." At much too young an age.

"Oh, I learned in college. I learned well."

He laughed again, not about to say that he'd been fifteen around Sammy, but he was pretty sure Bastian got the hint. "Anyway, that's the plan. Relax a little. I have boys to wrangle while you two are off on your adventure tomorrow."

"That stinks. You can take me on the next adventure and leave him with the boys."

"Just doing my job, ma'am." Ash winked at her and went to put his plate in the dishwasher. "I'm supposed to be looking after kids."

"You're good at it. I think you need to keep him on, Uncle Bastian."

"Do you?"

"Yes. I heard that it was only three months. That's not nice."

He was glad he was standing behind Bastian where they couldn't exchange any looks. "You've been listening in, huh?" Three months wasn't long; it was true. Just long enough to get Sammy settled in school and maybe make Halloween costumes.

"I'm not stupid. I don't have to eavesdrop." Her voice was flat.

"Well, I tell you what; I'll speak with Ash and see if he can sign a new contract, but if he has already been offered another job, that's that."

"You'd do that?" Sammy teared up, searching her uncle's face.

"I would. He's a good member of the family, don't you think?"

She nodded to Bastian.

"You two are going to make me cry." And he meant it. Bastian's words and Sammy's teary eyes made his chest ache. He did feel like part of the family, but he'd thought that was mostly in his own mind until dinner with Bastian the other night.

He'd signed a shorter contract in part because his last gig had been so many years long. He still kept in touch with them, got updates, the kids texted him... and he wasn't sure he was ready for another family. When he'd signed on with Bastian's mother, he wasn't even sure he wanted to be a nanny anymore. He'd been thinking more about what was next for him.

He reached across the table and took Sammy's hand. "I can stay longer, Sammy. Your uncle and I will talk about it."

She held on tight. "Thank you. We need you here. I'm starting a new school, art class, Girl Scouts, and all the Hs."

"All the Hs?"

"Uh-huh." She stared over at her uncle, who nodded.

"Four of them. Four Hs."

"Oh, is that the livestock thing? I think I've heard of it. You're going to be busy. I guess you will need some help."

Sammy nodded. "I will. And Uncle Bastian too. He's new at this whole kid thing."

Bastian tried not to smile; Ash saw it.

"It does seem like it." Ash took her plate away. "But he knows quiet time and bedtime. And it's that time for you, young lady."

She sighed, so dramatic. "I can't wait to grow up."

"Oh, honey. Be a kid while you can. Being a grown-up is overrated."

"I know you're eight going on eighteen, but trust me. Tap the brakes and just enjoy being young. All of us grown-ups would like to be eight again sometimes." Ash shooed her out of her chair. "You want to be tucked in? One of us can come up in an hour."

"Ninety minutes, please. I'm watching a movie. I promise to stay in bed, fair?"

"You're going to be a lawyer one day, Sammy." Bastian nodded and grinned at her.

"That's a deal, but only because it's summer. School rules will be different." Sammy *would* make an excellent lawyer. "Do they have lawyers in space?"

"I'm sure they do." Bastian went wide-eyed. "Court in Space?"

Sammy looked between them as she got up. "You are both very strange."

Ash didn't hold back his giggles as he chased her out of the kitchen. "Bed. Bed!"

She squealed and ran, and he loved it, the proof that she was a little girl, still.

Ash chased her up the stairs, and then the house went

quiet. He jogged back into the kitchen, still giggling. "I hear that you're new at this whole kid thing."

"I am. Brand new. I hear that you might be willing to stay and help." Bastian handed him a beer, offered him a warm smile.

"Did you see her face? How could I not be? She's terrified of anyone leaving her again, even me. I'll stay. She needs to get her feet back under her."

Bastian smiled at him. "I'm glad. We need you—all of us. I hope... I want you to be happy here."

The sincerity in that statement brought that ache back to his chest. He was happy here. He didn't have anywhere else to be. If he was needed, he'd stay. And if Bastian kept looking at him like that, he'd—

Ash blinked and tried not to blush, taking a long gulp of his beer to hide it.

Bastian glanced down, then back up, then down again.

"It's beautiful here. I love watching the sun go down. Do you want to go sit outside?" Outside, where they could watch the sun and not each other.

"Sounds perfect. I'll bring the pizza." Bastian grabbed the pizza box and his beer. "Get some paper towels?"

"You got it." He took the roll off the counter and followed Bastian out. They were laughing again as they maneuvered through the back door with their hands full.

"Lord have mercy, I do love this porch. I always have, since I can remember."

"This is a million-dollar view. I've never been anywhere like it. I love this time of day back here." It made him feel small. Not insignificant, just in perspective. The land was vast, the sky was endless, and he was just one little, tiny piece of it.

He could stare forever, no trees, no buildings that barred the view.

He glanced over at Bastian and then back at the colorful sunset. "I really do want to learn all those things we talked about—what you do, how to ride, everything. I wasn't sure how I was going to accomplish all of that in three months anyway."

"I can't imagine you leaving. You're... it's like you belong here."

He smiled. "It feels that way sometimes. It's hard to believe it's only been a couple of weeks." He felt like he'd walked into a space made just for him. He and Bastian could so easily have butted heads, but Bastian accepted his help right away.

"I needed help. I still—I mean, I slept five hours in a row last night. That's a miracle."

"The boys sleep like logs. All this air wipes them out."

Bastian tilted his head. "The air?"

"Sure. Fresh air, outdoor play, exercise? It's so good for them. Lots of healthy stimulation leads to deep, healthy sleep." He took a sip of his beer. "I've been sleeping pretty well myself."

"Good deal. I hope Sammy likes the school..."

"I hope so too. It was such a win to get her to agree to go see it, and then you get a gold star for your performance tonight. I was impressed with your negotiation skills." Bastian had Sammy's number now.

"I'm trying. God, I'm so trying to make her... if not happy, then willing to try, you know?" Bastian shook his head. "My mother keeps threatening to come and visit, take her school shopping."

"Let her. Kids have to learn how to relate to grandparents. It's a rite of passage." Ash nodded, thinking this was a great idea. "Plus, the more people Sammy has around her that love her, the better."

"Uh-huh. Her love is fierce. Like a wildfire."

"That's good. Sammy might relate to that." Sammy had fire in her too. "I'm looking forward to meeting your mother in person. She was great on the phone. Very direct, sure of what she needed."

"That's Mama. My dad is super chill. He just wants to ride horses, grill burgers, and play cards. Mama is a true Texas tornado." Bastian winked at him.

Ash laughed. "I'm sure I will like them both. When do they want to come? I can make up a bed. Do they have a room they usually stay in?"

"Anna will set them up. They stay on the main floor in their old bedroom. I figure it'll be theirs forever, right?" Bastian shrugged and chuckled. "I—It's weird. Parental relationships are weird."

"Are they?" Ash winked. "I seem to get along with parents." He loved that they still had their own bedroom that was theirs forever. That seemed so rare.

"You get along with me pretty well too. You play cards?"

There was no way Bastian was flirting with him; he was making all of that up in his head, reading too much into the smiles and the glances. Wishful thinking. "Go Fish? Crazy Eights? Slap Jack?" He flashed Bastian a goofy grin.

"Poker? Cribbage? Rummy?" Bastian winked at him. "I mean, you don't have to hang out with me, but we have a lot of evenings ahead of us."

"I do play grown-up cards too, yes." Ash laughed. "I want to hang out with you. I don't think I'll ever get tired of this view. I also like movies, and I can make about a hundred different kinds of cookies."

"No shit? Anna will be tickled shitless. She makes a great

biscochito, but that's really her cookie repertoire. I play video games, do weird metal art, and I love music."

"I love video games, but I am terrible at them. Maybe while your parents are here to distract the kids, you can show me your art?" He was so curious. It was a shame it was all put away, though he understood childproofing.

"Sure. It's... It's exciting, soldering things together, making things fit."

Ash didn't know if it would be exciting for him, but he could see in Bastian's eyes how much he loved it. "I can't wait."

"You know, man make fire. Rawr!" Bastian ducked his head, cheeks pinking.

He laughed. "So macho for a queer cowboy. Rar!"

"Oh, I am super macho. No question." Bastian flexed, so playful, but it was actually pretty hot.

"Look at you, all studly." Jesus. How did he let himself say that? He needed to stop thinking about his employer as hot.

"You should have seen Stephen. He was built like a bodybuilder. I'm more compact."

If that was compact, Stephen must have been enormous. "So, I have to ask a really inappropriate, possibly rude question. You absolutely don't have to answer it, okay? You can tell me off if you want to, but... I didn't think cowboys were allowed to be gay."

"Well, I mean—leather, chaps, boots..." Bastian ducked his head, cheeks blazing. "I mean, this isn't Texas. Folks pretty much leave each other alone, live their lives. Especially if the gay cowboy has a lot of money."

"Wait. Gay cowboys are kinky too?" Ash pretended to be shocked, hand on his chest.

"What?" Bastian's eyes went wide. "Do you know any?"

"I wish." He did a little happy dance in his seat.

"Ooo... look at you! I'm not the most kinky beast in the world, but I can ask around for you, on the downlow." Bastian winked at him. "Nanny searching for leather and lace on his time off."

"Ha! No!" He blushed hard. "No, I was kidding. I'm not—I don't—Oh Jesus." He laughed, shaking his head and hiding behind his beer.

Bastian cackled, the joy just ringing out. "Oh, that was something else, yessir."

"Shut up, evil cowboy." But even he had to admit that was pretty funny. He wouldn't have thought Bastian had such a good sense of humor, judging by the first day they'd met. But the cowboy even looked better now. Still tired but the dark circles had lightened up and Bastian smiled more.

A lot more. And he had an adorable smile.

"Oh, you've been talking to my niece. She agrees with you, all the way."

"Nah." Ash set his empty beer down. "She's just testing to make sure you love her no matter what."

"I'm just about ready to pass—I don't need an A, man."

"In this case, passing and an A are about the same thing, I think." The sun was down, and it was fully dark now. "How about that card game?"

"Let's do it. We can head to the game room. Come on."

"There's a game room?" How long had he been here? He had no idea there was a game room.

"Of course there is. I needed a room to play pool, didn't I?"

"Well, of course you did." He couldn't stop grinning. Bastian's parents must have done very well for themselves, but Bastian carried that torch well. He had money, but he worked hard too.

"It used to be my Abue's rooms, and I spent a lot of time playing in here, so when I took over the ranch, I made it my man cave." He led Ash over to a part of the house that he'd never explored and opened a huge purple door.

Man cave.

It was like a little fantasy—pool table, big screen with media chairs, a full-sized Pac-Man arcade game, and a dart board setup. Damn.

"Whoa. This is nice." He took it all in for a second, then pulled the baby monitor off his belt to make sure it worked in here, which it did just fine. "Gotta hear the boys."

"Yes. Sammy wakes up around three-thirty, usually."

"I keep hoping that will stop for her." It was going to take time. Distraction. He walked over to the poker table. "So, what are we playing?"

Bastian pulled out a cribbage board. "We'll work up to poker, huh?"

8

Bastian managed to get back to the ranch without screaming. Sammy had simply shorted out—she'd hated lunch, hated the school, refused to see the art studio.

So he drove her to the ranch without saying a word, even as she sat and sobbed, begging and pleading with him to bring her parents back.

He couldn't do this.

He just couldn't.

Ash was on the porch, coloring with the boys as he pulled up to the house, and Ash stood and gave them a wave and a big smile.

"I hate you. You will never be my family. You will never be my daddy!" She threw the door open. "I will never, ever like you! Ever."

He met Ash's gaze, waited until she slammed the door and ran to Ash, then he pulled off, leaving them all in a cloud of dust.

He needed help. He needed a friend. He—

"Siri, call Early."

"Calling Early Jericho."

Early was a ranch owner, a family man, and a longtime friend. The phone rang a couple of times before Early answered.

"Mr. Martindale!" Early sounded cheerful. "It's been ages. To what do I owe the pleasure?"

"I need help. I can't do this, man. I'm not dad material." He wasn't going to have to look Early in the eyes for months, so he could spill his guts.

"Okay. Hold on. I just need to—" There was some shuffling on Early's end and muffled voices, and then it got very quiet. "Tough day, huh?"

"God yes. Seriously. I took Sammy to see the school. I did everything that everyone said I was supposed to, and— she lost it!" Tears, hysteria, fury—the whole enchilada.

"Mm. Maybe a bit too much reality for her? Kids are unpredictable, and I can't imagine what she is going through right now. I'm sorry, man. What did you do?"

"I tried being calm. I tried showing her the art studio. I tried not yelling. I tried loving her. Nothing worked. She hates me. I left her with the nanny. I had to walk away." His heart was broken.

"Walking away was a good move. A little bit of space is probably good too. When Connor and I were first moving here, we were apart for a whole summer. I had the kids on my own, and they were having a good time, but they missed their dad. I let them take it out on me for a while because I felt terrible for them, but eventually I stopped that. I set a limit. It sounds like you're there. She's allowed to be upset, but you can remind her that you have feelings too."

"I mean... I never tried to be her dad. Shit, her dad and I spoke once a year at Christmas. That was it. We even texted on birthdays."

"You're the only parent-figure she has now. You don't

have to try. She's what? Eight, right? This isn't rational for her, it's emotional. But it sounds to me like you're doing what you need to be doing. Getting her back to normal life. Or as close to normal as possible."

"So, what about me? I'm…" He sighed and pulled around the back of one of the barns, head on the steering wheel. *Grow up, cowboy. What about him? He was the guardian of these babies.*

"You're only human, Bastian. You can't be perfect, and you can't be everything she needs. No one could. Is she in counseling?"

"I have us on a waiting list. I just don't think that the online thing is for an eight-year-old, you know? I mean, I still have another two weeks before a primary care can see them."

"Ah, it's tough with the underserved population down there." Early sighed. "That's hard. I think if I were you, I'd calmly let her know your feelings are hurt. That all you're doing is trying to help, and that you miss your brother too. Go through the motions, but let her sit with that for a while."

"Yeah. Yeah, I'm trying, man. I just—I just want to scream back. I want to throw something, you know?" He didn't. He *wouldn't.* He wasn't an asshole, but his soul hurt.

"You have a lot of land, Bastian. Go somewhere and do it. Scream it out. Or go bang some metal for a while and channel all that into a sculpture. Isn't that why you started building those damn things to start with?"

"Yeah, I guess. Once upon a time. Maybe I will. Maybe I'll just lock myself in the studio for an hour or three." He needed to call Ash first.

"A wise man, otherwise known as my husband, once told

me that you can't take care of others unless you take care of yourself first. It's good advice."

"Yeah. Well, I'm trying to just... not lose my motherfucking mind." It was a close thing.

"That's a good goal. Lean on the nanny more if you need to." Early chuckled. "I assume that's why you hired them. To help."

"Him, and I didn't hire him to begin with, but I have... I've asked him to stay."

"Good choice. You need the help. Who hired him to start with, your mother? Smart woman. I'm sure you didn't realize how tough kids can be. They're a challenge under the best of circumstances."

"Yeah. I just was... I didn't know what I needed. I didn't know anything." Not anything at all.

"It's not easy, man. It's just not. And you have it tougher than most. Be patient with yourself."

"I'm trying. I've never done anything so hard." Or so wrong.

"Nope, you never have. And there's no manual for the hard stuff. But you're a good man with a lot to give those kids. One day not too long from now, Sammy will smile at you, and all of this will have been worth it. I promise."

"If it isn't, I'm going to blame you, okay?" He was—mostly—teasing.

Early laughed gently. "I will take full and absolutely no responsibility."

He laughed, and that let a little of the horrible tension ease. "Thanks, man. I appreciate it."

"You're fine, man. For whatever it's worth, it's normal, all of that frustration. Walking away, getting some perspective was the right thing to do. Your instincts are spot-on. I don't have girls, but I've been through similar with both boys.

One day, I'm their best friend; the next, everything is *so unfair*."

"So, so very incredibly unfair. Yes. God. And you don't have girls *yet*." He knew they were trying.

"We shall see! It won't be long now. I'll send you a cigar. Do guys still do that? Cigars?"

"Nope. Send a text. I'll send Starbucks." That was easier.

"You got it. Call me any time, okay? Like any time. I'm about to be up at three a.m. a lot." Early chuckled.

"You know it. Thanks, bro. I owe you." And he knew Early would take him up on it.

"Good to hear your voice. Take care." Early hung up, leaving just him and his truck and the quiet.

He needed to text Ash, he guessed, and as soon as his hands stopped shaking, he did.

BASTIAN

I'm okay. Just needed a break

It took a minute, but he got an answer.

ASH

Take all the time you need. We're okay too.

BASTIAN

Good. She had a rough day

And that was an understatement.

ASH

You too, sounds like. She's quiet now.

BASTIAN

Good. Going to the shed to set shit on fire.

ASH

Rar! Be studly. I've got this. Also there are
cookies when you get back.

BASTIAN

Cool. I'll be a couple

He needed to bang and burn. He needed to scream a
little.

He needed to reset his brain.

9

Bastian didn't make it to dinner, so he'd either set himself on fire or was in some kind of metal-banging trance.

Or he'd had some whiskey and was passed out in the barn.

Ash figured any of the above was legit after the day Bastian had.

The boys were so freaked out by Sammy's rage they went to bed easily, very ready to get out of her sphere. Sammy took the longest shower ever, said goodnight, and closed her door.

He took the goodnight as a good sign and gave Sammy her space.

There was a light in one of the barns, and periodically he could hear the thump of furious music.

Jesus, those two must have had an absolutely vicious day.

He wandered into the kitchen where Anna was cleaning up for the evening. "So... do I leave him alone, or go check on him?"

She handed him a huge water bottle, a sandwich, and a Dr Pepper. "Water first, then food. I'll stay here with Wylie until y'all are back, fair?"

That was exactly what he'd hoped she'd say. He was more anxious about Bastian than he was about Sammy. "Thank you, Anna." He picked up the food and drinks. "I'll try not to be too long. I'm sure he's exhausted."

"We're fine here. Just feed him. He'll need a friend."

He nodded to her and headed out the back door. It wasn't dark yet, which was good because there were critters out here at night that would probably love the sandwich he was carrying.

He walked in through the barn door, following the light and the loud music. He still didn't know exactly what had happened; Sammy hadn't had much to say. She and Bastian were equally furious with each other though. That was obvious.

The sound of banging and pounding rang out, filling the air. The door wasn't closed, so he swung it open, peeking in.

The "studio" was a huge building, filled with bins and barrels of metal. The walls were lined with sculptures—a T-rex, a huge salmon, a gigantic moose, and vast flowers.

"Whoa..." The banging barely registered as he wandered into the open room, moving around the sculptures, eyes roaming the walls. "These are yours?"

"Y-yeah. Hey. Come on in." Bastian was shirtless, sweating, black streaks covering him.

"They're amazing." Holy shit, the man was hot. He handed Bastian the water right away and tried not to stare at the cowboy's muscled chest and arms.

"Thanks." Bastian sucked down half the bottle, then poured the rest over the top of his head.

"Mhm. Anna sent a sandwich. She's staying a bit to keep an ear out for the kids."

"Yeah? Cool. Have a seat. There's a bunch of feed sacks over there." Bastian pointed to a weird pile of fabric. "It's solid."

He handed Bastian the sandwich and set down the Dr Pepper, then tested out the feed sacks. Not too bad. "How are you feeling?"

"Better. I needed to work some shit out. How's Sammy?"

"I'm not sure. Raw. Exhausted. She didn't say much. She let me sit with her until she settled down though."

"Good. I swear, I didn't do anything to her. I was good. I wanted it to be good."

"No. I'm sure you didn't. Something overwhelmed her or scared her. Maybe it was just too real, you know? I started to ask, but I thought better of it. She'll say when she's ready." He hadn't wanted to push at all. She just wanted him to be present with her, and she wasn't ready to talk.

"We were fine until she walked into the school, and it just dissolved." Bastian looked as devastated as Sammy had.

Ash nodded. "Maybe she needs to be home-schooled. At least for now. I can set that up for her." This wasn't something that was going to work itself out in a week.

"I don't... I don't think so. Doesn't she need to go? Doesn't she need to try?" Bastian sat on the floor with a thump.

"That depends on why she wigged out, I guess." He agreed. He'd like to see Sammy make some friends, get out of the house. But if she physically couldn't do it, if the fear or grief was that strong, they might have to get creative.

"I don't know, man. Maybe I'll take her to a *doctor*-doctor, get her checked out."

"Couldn't hurt. Maybe I'll try to run her up to school

again in a couple of days too." He didn't think it would be any different with him there, but it was worth a shot. "I'm hoping she'll say something, give one of us an opening to ask what happened."

"Yeah, I hope. Maybe it is just me. Maybe I'm just too close to family."

"Could be. Could be that you turned just so and she saw her father in you. Could be anything. But she was so excited to go with you, and she seemed so ready."

"She did. She was chatty and happy until we walked in!"

"Did someone say something? Did she see something?"

"It's just a school, man. Mascot. Trophies. Pictures. It was just a school. The kids aren't there. The teachers were. There's a playground—normal school shit."

He sighed, searching his mind for any kind of rational explanation. "Do you know if her dad used to take her to school in the morning?"

"I don't. We weren't close, Ash. He wasn't a fan of the cowboy life, and he thought we were crazy for staying out here in the high desert."

He nodded. "Right. I'm sorry. I'm just grasping at anything I can think of. We'll have to hope she says something tomorrow."

"I just—I want her to be okay. Just a normal kid, you know?"

Sammy didn't seem like an average eight-year-old, but he understood what Bastian meant. More than that, he could hear real emotion in the cowboy's words. Real love for Sammy. "I know. I want that for her too. I think she wants that for herself, and that might be what gets us all through this."

"I hope so. I just love them all, and the boys are okay.

They're both going to be okay, but Sammy's so goddamn mad."

Ash felt like angry was better than withdrawn. He had to believe that as long as Sammy was letting herself feel something, she was moving in a good direction. "She's not mad at you. That's important to remember, I think. You're the one here to listen, but it's not you she's angry with."

"Do you think so?" Poor Bastian was devastated; it was written on his face.

"Hey." He got up and moved closer to rest a comforting hand on Bastian's shoulder. "She's not mad at you; she's mad at the universe. You didn't do this to her. She knows that."

"I didn't. I'd give anything to get them back, I swear to God." Bastian's dark eyes filled with tears, and he took a shaky breath.

"It's okay. You're okay." He hugged Bastian impulsively, not sure what else to do.

"I'm not. I'm so fucking worried about her. I want her to be able to grow up like a normal girl."

He sighed and rubbed Bastian's back. "You can only do your best. She has lots of years to grow up. This is just one point in time. One challenge. There will be dozens as she grows up. You have to take it a day at a time."

"Yeah. I just need to stop hoping things will be okay."

"You need to hope tomorrow is going to be okay. And don't think any farther than that right now. You'll worry yourself sick." He hugged Bastian tighter, finding he felt as worried about the cowboy as he was about Sammy.

Bastian gasped as he fought to breathe, and Ash held him, offering him support, peace, he hoped.

Bastian had been trying too hard, putting so much of himself into making things all right for these kids. And it was easy to forget that Bastian was grieving too, even if it was only for a relationship he now could never have with his brother.

"I never wanted this. I never wanted him dead. I wanted to be his friend, man!"

Part of Ash wanted to tell Bastian to stop, but another part of him knew Bastian needed this.

"I know," he whispered. He knew what losing family felt like, even if his wasn't actually dead. "You didn't have control over that either."

"No. I'm free-falling, but I thought—I thought I was doing better."

"You are. This is one bad day after a string of good ones. It's okay. Just accept it. Breathe."

"Yeah. Right. In and out." Bastian sucked in a lungful of air and blew it out.

He just held on, loosening his grip a little as Bastian started to relax. "Parenting is hard. This is harder. You have to stay the course and let yourself do this sometimes."

"I'm sorry, man. I didn't mean to fall out all over you." Bastian blushed dark pink. "Honest."

"No apologies. Actually, it was good. I was starting to worry you really might set this barn on fire." He chuckled softly, trying to lighten things up a little. "You're only human."

"No shit on that. I'm not sure I'm good at it, but I am, all the way." Bastian's laugh rang out. "And that didn't make a lick of sense."

He found he was reluctant to let go of Bastian, the cowboy was so solid and warm, but he did before it got weird and went back to his pile of sacks to sit. "I understood it anyway."

"Thank God for small favors." Bastian chuckled and shook his head, coming to sit next to him.

He glanced over and gave Bastian's knee a pat. "Are you ready to head back inside?"

"Yeah. Yeah, I want a shower, supper, to see the kids."

"Kids are in bed. The boys snuggled hard and crashed early—I think Sammy had them anxious. And she's behind closed doors, but maybe we can peek in."

"I won't bother her. She doesn't want to see me."

Ash knew that would change in the middle of the night when there would be night terrors and no one but her uncle could soothe them.

"Come on. Bring your sandwich, and we'll get you a shower and a beer." He stood and offered Bastian a hand up.

"Thank you for coming out. What do you think of my new piece?"

He glanced over, then blinked. It was a horse. A running horse.

He hadn't really looked at it until now.

"Bastian... that is incredible." He took a tour around it, looking up and down. He was more than impressed; he was a little awed. "It's beautiful."

"Thank you. It's a hobby, but I find it a good workout."

"I bet it is. And a good outlet, it seems, too. Who doesn't want to beat the shit out of something once in a while?" He held Bastian's sandwich as the cowboy closed up the barn.

"You know it. Hammering. Burning. Bending. It's magic. You got hobbies besides kicking my ass at cribbage?"

"Uh. Reading? Watching movies. Baking cookies. Not really." He laughed. "I seem to either not have free time or end up wasting it when I do. But I want to add horseback riding and maybe gardening to my list."

"You want to put in a garden in the spring? Or hell, get someone to put in a greenhouse. I don't care. I'd do that."

"I don't know. I know nothing about gardening and even

less about what grows here or when. But I think it would be fun. Work, but fun. And the kids could help. I guess I should do some research."

He'd have to get the kids in on it because if and when they decided it was time for him to move on, he'd want someone to know what to do with it. He still didn't know what "stay" meant. A year? Two? Ten?

Fifteen? Could he stay here for fifteen years and leave? He wasn't sure he could do that again. It was hard enough after his last gig, and he'd known that was coming for two years.

He bumped elbows with Bastian. "Kicking your ass at cribbage is a pretty good hobby though."

"Yeah yeah yeah. I intend to let you win for the first year or so, then it's my turn for a while."

He gasped. "Let me—oh, hell no. I'll have none of that, cowboy. I don't need your pity."

"No?" Bastian actually laughed for him, and he smiled as they walked in.

Anna and Wylie came right to them, giving Bastian hugs and support.

And beer.

Sammy was complicated, but even if he weren't standing here, Bastian was far from alone and definitely not lacking in people who cared about him.

Daylight would be telling, but Ash felt like it was going to be okay.

For all of them.

10

"Help me! They're coming to hurt me!" The scream had Bastian bolting out of his bed, hitting Sammy's door like a freight train. "Uncle Bas! Uncle Bas, *PLEASE!*"

"Here, baby girl. I'm right here." He scooped her up, rocking her gently. His heart was pounding like a caffeinated squirrel, slamming in his chest. "I'm right here. No one's going to hurt you. I promise to God."

"Why are they doing that? Why? I didn't wish for *that*." She clutched at his chest, shaking like a leaf.

And it wasn't a second later that Ash appeared in the doorway.

"No one's going to hurt you. I promise you. I will not let anyone hurt you. Neither will Ash. You are safe right here."

"They're going to have to get through us, Sammy. You're safe. I promise." Ash came in, laid a hand on his shoulder, kissed the top of Sammy's head. "Sorry to interrupt, but that scream—I'll leave you two alone. Call me if you need me."

"No. No, stay." Sammy sniffled. "Can you watch the door?"

She held onto him, though. She wasn't leaving his arms.

"I promise you're safe. They're not coming for you. They love you. They're loving you from heaven."

"I can. I will." Ash retreated a few steps and lingered near the doorway. "I'm right here."

"Why are they so ugly and mean in my dream, then?" Sammy sniffled and took a hitching breath.

"Because you're mad at them, and you feel bad that you're angry, maybe?" He just knew that this sort of thing seemed to make sense.

"I was mad at them when they left," Sammy mumbled. "They were supposed to be at my piano recital at school, but Daddy had a party at work, and Mommy said she had to go." Sammy wiped her nose with the sleeve of her nightgown, and Ash appeared out of nowhere with a Kleenex. "They were supposed to come home after dinner, and I was going to do a concert just for them."

Sammy sat up a little and looked him right in the eye, and there was the anger he'd seen in her eyes at school earlier. "They shouldn't have gone out at all!"

"No, they shouldn't have. They should have been at your concert." He didn't even know that she played piano. He'd be at all her things, even if she didn't want him there.

She nodded, and the anger slipped away, leaving her looking so sad. "Do you think they hate me because I was mad?"

"No." That was the easiest answer, and the truth too. "That's not how love works. They loved you more than anything. Nothing you could have done would ever make them hate you. I swear to you. You are safe, and you are loved, and if you are mad, I understand. I will love you no matter what." Because she was his family. Because Stephen had trusted him. Because she was Sammy.

"They should have been at my recital. Then they

wouldn't have been in the car. Why didn't they just come to my recital? That's why I'm still mad. If they'd just—UGH! WHY!?" Sammy pounded on his chest, but it wasn't anywhere near hard enough to hurt him.

He let her beat on him, keeping her safe, but not stopping her. It couldn't hurt for her to work this out.

She finally sighed and slumped against him. "I hate not knowing why."

"Me too. It sucks so hard. I wish I had answers for both of us." He didn't hide his own confusion and sorrow.

"I want them to stop being so mean in my dreams."

"Do you know about dreamcatchers? I can ask my godfather Ezra to pick us one up. His lady, Aria, she makes them. They're made to stop bad dreams. They have good energy, and Aria would put all the wonderful wishes into it."

"They stop bad dreams? For real?" Sammy peered at him.

"They have been used in this area for a long time. Ezra brought me one when I was a little boy. It's still in my bedroom."

"And you don't have bad dreams?" Sammy bit her lip, looking hopeful.

"Not very often at all. Just the way that I knew someone cared enough to make me one makes me feel better, you know?"

Sammy nodded. "I think that would be nice, then. I like the name Aria too."

"I've heard of dreamcatchers. I think they're supposed to be magical." Ash's voice floated into the room from the doorway.

"I know that they are important, and I know I believe that is good energy. You want me to call Ezra in the morning?"

"Would you?"

"Yes. Do you want me to put mine in here for you for now? I will."

She glanced over at Ash and then back at him. "Yes, please."

"Okay. I'll get it. You need to go to the bathroom or anything?"

"Yes. And blow my nose."

Ash took a step closer. "I can walk with you if you want."

Sammy nodded. "Okay."

Ash held out a hand and she took it.

"I'll grab the dreamcatcher and hang it up in here." Bastian headed to the bedroom where it was hanging and eased it off the wall before taking it to Sammy's room and finding a spot for it.

Sammy wandered back in with Ash behind her. "It's pretty. It looks like a spider web."

"That looks great right there."

"The dreams are supposed to get trapped in the web." He helped Sammy back into bed. "Those dreams aren't the truth. They're bad winds. Your folks love you. I swear it."

Sammy settled into the covers, looking as exhausted as she must have felt. "Bad winds." She held her arms up for a hug.

"That's right. Just bad winds. I love you, Sammy."

"I love you, Uncle Bas. I'm sorry. I just... I was so excited, and then I was so mad at them for messing things up."

"We'll try again. We've got this, girlfriend. You and me and Ash."

Sammy nodded and held out an arm. "Ash?"

"Hey, we've got this. One day at a time." Ash gave her a hug as well and tucked her in. "Sleep well, Sammy."

"No bad winds. Good night."

"Goodnight, Sammy." Ash headed for the bedroom door.

"Night. Holler if you need me." He headed out too, needing a drink more than anything.

Ash was waiting for him in the hallway, a dark shadow except where a little ambient light caught Ash's blue eyes. "You okay?"

Fuck no. "I need a drink. You wanna?"

Ash nodded. "Lead the way."

They ended up in the man cave, and he poured them both a finger of whiskey. "You need ice?"

"Sure."

He plopped a cube in the glass and handed it to Ash, only then noticing that Ash was only wearing pajama bottoms.

Damn, that was... a pretty belly. Softly fuzzy, leading to a trail to heaven.

"I don't think I've ever heard her scream like that. The dreamcatcher was a brilliant idea."

"I hope it helps. If she can sleep, she'll feel better, right?" Rest was important and helped her to be more emotionally stable.

"I think we all will." Ash sipped his drink. "You're really good with her. I know she's frustrating and exhausting, but you're helping."

"I hope so." He wasn't sure. He didn't know what to believe, so he believed he'd have another drink.

Ash stuck his out as he was pouring. "I got out of bed so fast, but you were faster. Impressive."

"I think I was waiting for her to call." He shrugged, letting the whiskey burn all the way down. "I couldn't settle at all."

"You need more sleep too. You can't cope without sleep.

Maybe we should trade off nights or something." Ash sat in one of the leather-back poker chairs and put his bare feet up on the poker table.

"Maybe, but... it kills me, hearing that fear." He couldn't sleep through that. No way.

Ash nodded, looking into his glass. "Yeah. I get that. And I don't usually hear her."

"It's awful. This is awful. I hate all this." He just wanted to grab hold of Ash and hug him.

"Hey." Ash stood again, setting his glass down. "Take a deep breath."

"I'm okay." No, he wasn't. "I'm trying to be okay."

"I know." Ash was standing in front of him quietly and reached out to take his glass from him. "You should go to bed."

"I know. I'm sorry. I'm trying."

Ash allowed him to finish off the drink, took his glass, and set it down, then put a hand on his shoulder, pushing gently. "Bed."

"Yeah. Yeah, I can do that." He swallowed hard, because he wanted to ask Ash to come with him.

Ash followed him out of the room and down the dark hallway to his bedroom and lingered in the doorway. "Are you good?" He could just make out a smile in the half-light. "Do you need me to tuck you in?"

"Hush. I just—I'm going to take a shower and see if I can't... chill. You'll listen for her?"

"I'll listen for her. Do what you need to do." Ash retreated from the doorway into the hall. "Get some sleep."

"You too. I—thank you. For everything."

He reached out, squeezed Ash's hand, and then stepped back into the room.

God, what was he doing? Flirting with the nanny?

"Uh-huh. Sure. Sleep well." He could hear Ash's bare feet in the hall as Ash hurried away.

"You too, honey." He needed to jack off and sleep. He'd be better off in the morning.

He had to be better off in the morning.

11

Ash sat at the picnic table with his feet up on a plastic chair and a bottle of water in one hand watching the boys splash around in the kiddie pool.

His eyes were dutifully on the boys, but his mind was everywhere else.

Bastian and Sammy had driven off this morning for another try at visiting her school, and he'd been thinking about them almost non-stop. Almost. Because when he wasn't worried about them, he was thinking about Bastian in ways he knew he shouldn't.

Bastian kept watching him, those dark eyes following him everywhere he went. It was maddening and fascinating and hotter than hell.

He wasn't an idiot. He understood what was happening, and he knew Bastian had to as well. But why there was a pull between them, and whether it was a good idea, stopped him from letting himself even think something between them was a possibility.

Bastian was in a bad place. Ash was helpful and

supportive. Bastian was possibly the only gay cowboy on the planet, and they were in the middle of nowhere.

"Ass?" Walt waved to him. "Play?"

"Ash, Walt."

"Asswall!"

His lips twitched as he tried not to grin, or even worse, laugh. "Asher. Is that easier?" He picked up a ball and tossed it into the little pool.

"Asher! Asher Asher Asher!" Walt splashed to get the ball.

Much better than Ass. He reached down and poked Will in the tummy. "Are you floating, Will?"

"Foaty?" Will grinned at him. "Sisser and Tio coming?"

"Soon, I hope. Sammy is learning all about her new school, and then they'll be home again." He hoped it would be soon. They'd been gone longer than last time, but was that a good sign or a bad one?

He caught the ball Walt whipped at him and tossed it back into the pool. That kid was going to be a pitcher.

"Asher!" Walt was so pleased, and the ball came winging.

He dove for it and managed to catch it without falling on his face. "Got it!" He tossed it back again, making sure it splashed in the water this time.

Both boys went after it, clunking heads with a thud.

Oh lord, the tears were imminent.

"Boing!" He tried to lighten things up before the bawling started. "You guys have hard heads!" He held his breath, already working on his strategy should this swim session go to hell.

"Boing?" Walt sniffled.

"Bwoing?" Will echoed.

"Boing!" He laughed and playfully bounced his forehead off his palm. "You bounced right off each other!"

If this worked, he deserved an Academy Award.

The boys started giggling, and then he heard the sound of a truck coming down the road, dust flying.

"They're home," he said softly, the words meant only for himself. Then he repeated it louder. "Tio's home. Let's find your towels."

"Tio! Sisser!" The boys jumped and splashed, so happy to see them.

Please, let this be... not awful.

The truck came to a stop, and it looked like they were screaming at each other in the cab.

Shit, shit, shit. Okay... get the boys inside and occupied. "Come on, guys, let's get towels."

Damn. Sammy'd seemed so brave this morning.

The engine cut off, and Sammy hopped out. "I love that song, Uncle Bas!"

"Get your stuff, girl. You bought the whole store!"

Sammy put one hand on her hip. "We can afford it."

He froze for a second, blinking in their direction. That didn't sound like World War III. It sounded like two very happy people.

He took a breath and tried not to look as surprised as he felt. "Did you have a good time?" he called out, drying off wiggly boys.

She started pulling bags out of the truck, talking a mile a minute. "I went to the art school first, and then went to meet my teacher. Her name is Señorita Douglas, and she was so sweet. She says that there are all sorts of activities, and we have skiing for PE in the winter! I love to ski. I didn't know there was skiing here!"

"That's amazing!" He glanced at Bastian, who looked a

little worn out but in a good way and gave him a wink. "Is the school big?"

"Not too big, but there's a playground and a cafeteria and a gym and an art room." She beamed at him. "Art school is Tuesday and Thursday afternoons, Girl Scouts is Wednesday, and Uncle Bas says he'll find a piano teacher and a piano just for me."

He finished drying Will off and let him run, then went after Walt, wrapping the boy in another towel. "I can't wait to hear you play. And all those activities! You must be so excited. I'm glad you like your teacher. School starts on Monday, huh?"

School started much earlier in New Mexico than in New York, where nothing happened until after Labor Day.

"Yeah, and we bought all my school supplies. Uncle Bas said I could choose everything and—" She just jabbered at him, and Bastian just followed behind with Target bags.

He herded the boys along, who seemed perfectly happy to listen to Sammy jabber, and he kept throwing smiles over his shoulder at Bastian as they took her haul up to her room. "Did you need lunch? Or are you going to get your things together for school?"

"I have to organize. We bought things for the twins and for you, but I'll bring them down." She shooed them out. "Go. Get dressed, boys."

"Oh. We're going. Off we go!" He laughed and shooed the boys toward their rooms, sending Walt with Bastian. "Naps in Walt's room?"

"No naps!" Will shook his head. "Tio! Play!"

"No naps?" Bastian's eye went wide, comical. "But how can you wake up and get presents if you don't nap?"

Oh, Bastian was learning. "I guess they don't want presents."

"I want presents! pjs for naps!" Will took off for his own room.

Walt sighed. "*Paw Patrol*?"

"After naps, son." Bastian nuzzled Walt's neck, blowing a gentle raspberry.

"We'll meet you in Walt's room." Really, the boys should just share a room. They were always together, even sleeping.

He got Will dressed, which took no time since Will was highly motivated to get this nap over with, and he jogged after Will back to Walt's room.

Walt was in Bastian's arms, thumb in his mouth, almost asleep. He opened his arms to his twin, and they settled in together.

He adored these boys; they were so sweet to each other and so stubbornly different. Ash helped Bastian extract himself and covered the boys up with a blanket.

Bastian stood up, dark eyes just twinkling merrily. Oh, someone was happy.

He kept quiet until they were out the door and made sure they were most of the way down the stairs before he spoke. "Nothing says success like school supplies."

"Going to the art school first seemed to help. She was more relaxed, man. More at peace with herself." Bastian stopped and hugged him tight, dropped a kiss on his lips.

He met Bastian's gaze and couldn't do much more than blink at him for a second as his body warmed from his toes to his ears. He knew he was blushing, and he opened his mouth like he should say something, but nothing came out.

Was that a celebratory oops, a truthful accident, or on purpose? How was he supposed to know? And was it okay? He'd just spent all week trying to convince himself it wasn't, but in the moment, it felt really fucking good.

Ash caught Bastian's fading smile and saw the

uncertainty start to creep into those dark eyes and did the only thing he could think of since his brain had shorted out. He kissed Bastian back, sliding his arms around the cowboy to return the hug.

Bastian's smile felt amazing against him, warm and happy, and they eased apart instead of jerking, which felt even better.

"I've been thinking about this all week, and I kept telling myself no."

Bastian nodded, catching his gaze. "Me too. I don't want you to think I'm taking advantage."

"I don't want you to think I am homing in on your family." He shrugged. "Or your money. Or worry the kids."

"Yeah. We'll have to be... mindful about how we move forward, hmm?"

He liked that Bastian said "move forward." It validated how Ash was feeling, and he felt okay talking about the future, at least in the short term. "I like you, a lot. Under other circumstances, I would jump right in here with both feet. But I don't want to break their hearts again." Like seemed inadequate, but anything more felt like he was rushing things.

"Fair enough. I just—it's been a great day, and I couldn't resist."

"You deserved a win. I'm glad you didn't resist." He dared to take Bastian's hand. "Snack? Beer?"

"Yes, on the snack. I'll wait until tonight for my beer. I don't like drinking when the kids are awake."

"Have you tried the oatmeal cookies I made yet?" Really, he just wanted another kiss.

"Ooh... oatmeal cookies rock. Can we have peanut butter next?" Bastian danced him around for a second. "She did it, man. She did it."

He laughed and went with it, enjoying the playful part of Bastian he hadn't seen much of yet. "I knew she could. I *knew* it."

"She did. It's not the end of things, I know, but—" Bastian shrugged. "It's a great start."

"One day at a time. We know the next day will be hard, right?" The first day of school could be tough no matter what the circumstances, but it would be a dose of reality for Sammy. "Hopefully, it will be so fun she won't have time to worry. I assume her teachers know what's going on?"

"Yes, and so does the principal. They say that it's more common than you'd think to have children that are living with guardians, who have suffered losses. They have a counselor available for her too. Like a real one."

"That's good news. I mean, we're awesome, but I don't know if we're enough." At some point, Sammy would need someone who wasn't family. He was sure.

Bastian nodded to him. "I'm not one of those folks that's all, no headshrinkers! She's had a bunch of blows at once, and I can't help her with how she hates it here, because this place is my whole life."

"Hate is a strong word. I think she liked Connecticut. Anywhere else will take time to feel like home. The more you show her why you love it, the more she will too." He kissed Bastian's cheek. "It's definitely working on me."

"Yeah? Good. This is my heaven. I want everyone to see it, fall in love."

So far, so good.

And he was not going to say that out loud.

Not.

"You had me at the view." He smiled and then glanced away because that wasn't any better. That might actually have been worse to say.

"I was thinking about grilling burgers tonight for supper. There are hot dogs for the twins. You got something you like with it? I have stuff for queso…"

"Ooh. Hot cheese please. Are you grilling veggies?" He led Bastian into the kitchen and handed him a cookie.

Bastian took the cookie and snapped it up. "Sure. I have bell peppers, calabacitas, mushrooms…"

"I love a cookout. Just tell me what I can do." He stood close to Bastian, closer than he'd ever dared before today. "But maybe another kiss first?"

"Oh, I can manage that. Another kiss. This one, planned." And Bastian leaned down, bringing their lips together.

Oh, planned was better. Bastian's kiss was full of confidence and curiosity, and he slipped an arm around Bastian's waist and leaned in.

Bastian didn't swallow him, but the kiss wasn't chaste, either, keeping his focus until he heard Sammy's feet on the stairs.

Even so, he broke it off gently, smiling. "Later, cowboy. Have another cookie."

"Sounds like a plan to me. I love cookies." Bastian's smile was… pure heat.

Sammy stopped in front of both of them. "I would like a snack please."

"Cookie?" Ash picked up the plate and offered it to her. "Organizing for school is hungry work, hm?"

"Yes. Here are the school things for the twins. I think you need them."

"Oh." He took the bags from Sammy and glanced at Bastian. "I guess I'm homeschooling the boys?"

"Well, they are three…" Bastian grinned at him. "They have another two years."

"Or one and then preschool." He winked at Bastian. "I am a big believer in preschool. So what do I have here, Sammy? Numbers? Letters? Crayons?"

"I found you pre-K schoolbooks, numbers and letters, colors, and blocks."

"Perfect." First, he'd have to teach them to sit still. That could take a month all by itself. "You're so sweet to look after them."

"They're my brothers." She shrugged, then glanced at Bastian. "Can I give him his present?"

"Sure, honey."

She handed him a bag that had a couple of video games and a gorgeous fluffy scarf. "It gets cold here."

"Oh my goodness. This is so kind." He put the bags down, pulled out the scarf, and wrapped it around his neck, smiling at the thoughtfulness and also how much it made him feel like family. "I love it. Thank you. Hug?" He held his arms open.

"Sure!" Sammy hugged him. "I need to get my clothes all ready."

"Did you pick out a first-day outfit?"

"Not yet. I'm still working on that. but it's a surprise anyway, so you don't get to see." Sammy seemed very sure of herself, but he was concerned about first-day-of-school tears.

"How about I consult, and we make it a surprise for Uncle Bastian? Because everyone needs a fashion consultant, right?"

She tilted her head. "But Uncle Bas is gay, sorta like the *Queer Eye* guys. Doesn't that mean he'd be better at it?"

His lips twitched and he smiled. He didn't see any reason to not be out in this house. "Funny you say that, because I just told your uncle that I am gay too."

"O. M. G. For reals?" Her eyes went wide as saucers.

He laughed because that was adorable. "For really reals."

"Wow. That's cool, because Uncle Bas isn't a very good gay. Gay... person? Gay man?" She flipped one hand. "He doesn't do his hair, he doesn't moisturize, and he—have you seen his clothes?"

He glanced at Bastian, who looked both confused and amused, and worked very hard not to laugh.

It was almost impossible.

"He's a hardworking guy. He doesn't want to get his nice clothes dirty. He's got a great hat though."

"Uh-huh. And he can *shop*."

Bastian turned away, shoulders shaking hard with laughter.

"Well, then he's not a totally bad gay person." He giggled. He had to let some of it out, or he'd explode. "So. I get to help and we can surprise him. Yes?"

"Okay. No peeking, Uncle."

"You have my word, Sobrina."

"Gracias," she shot back, and Bastian grinned.

"De nada."

"I can't wait." He gave her a big squeeze and sent her on her way, watching from the kitchen door as she hurried through the foyer and up the stairs. Then he turned and grinned at Bastian, who was practically purple. "Are you really a terrible gay?"

"Awful. I mean, I manscape, but that's about it."

Dude, Bastian managed that with a straight face.

"Clearly you need more sequins in your life." He stepped in close again. "Maybe on your hat."

"Yeah? I think not. I'm not a sequin guy."

"No. You're not. And next time I'm trying not to laugh,

how about a little solidarity?" He laughed. "I thought you were going to bust something."

"Jesus, I did too. She was killing me with her moisturizers." Bastian leaned against one of the chairs, cackling again.

"Are you dry? Let me see." Ash took Bastian's face in his hands and slid his fingers over Bastian's cheeks. "You seem okay to me."

"Not too many eye wrinkles?" Bastian squinted, playing with him.

"Just the right amount. Especially when you smile."

"Hola. Tomorrow, I am cooking so I am dropping off a few things." Anna came right in the kitchen door with groceries, and Ash had no idea what to do. He dropped his hands and took a step back, crossing his arms over his chest.

Bastian chuckled. "Anything yummy? Anything I love?"

"No, spoiled man. I'm making liver and onions."

Bastian made gagging noises.

Was it wrong that he just wanted the kitchen to themselves again? He loved Anna. But he wanted to touch Bastian a little more.

Instead, he focused on his job. "If you're looking for something to talk with Sammy about, you could ask her what she wants for lunch on her first day of school. Her visit went well today."

"Oh, thank God. I've been praying for that. Can I go up and see her? Hear about her day?"

"Sure, lady. The boys are napping, but she's in her room."

Ash helped her put the groceries away. He wasn't sure what she was going to make, but there was a lot of cheese.

"I will be back." Anna gave a wave and headed for the stairs.

"What needs that much cheese?"

"Uh...queso flaemado?"

"I don't know what that is, but anything with cheese works for me." Ash pulled out his phone to google it.

Oh, damn. Flaming cheese.

That sounded amazing and incredibly not twin-friendly.

"Wow. She's going to set Will on fire." Ash stuffed his phone back in his pocket.

"We'll let Will and Walt have cheese roll-ups. I used to love those when I was a kid."

"Sounds good." He leaned against the counter. "I'm running out of small talk."

"Do we need small talk?" The question was asked so gently, almost sweetly.

"No." God, he knew he was smiling like a loon and probably blushing too. He was such a dork. "We don't."

"Good." Bastian squeezed his hand. "You'd better go see your fashion show. I'm going to get the meat ready for tonight's supper."

"Careful, Mr. Macho Cowboy. You might prove Sammy right."

"Moi? Most likely. You never know about me."

"That is true." But hopefully, he'd know more very soon.

12

The burgers and queso had gone over well, and the boys managed their baths with only a few bits of drama.

Bastian even got Sammy to try the chile con queso without running or tears.

Ash was reading the boys a second book, holding up his end of the deal he'd made so Walt would let him wash his hair.

At some point, he was going to have to get the twins a haircut.

Maybe in three or four years...

Not yet.

"Tio!" Ash called from Walt's room.

"Tio! Kisses!" The boys echoed.

"Sobrinitos! Los amo!" He came into the room with a grin.

"Te amamos tambien!" they answered, in unison. Such good boys.

Ash tucked them in and moved over so he could give kisses. "Goodnight, chicos."

"Ni-night!"

Bastian gave both boys their kisses, rubbing their noses together. "Love you, beasts. I'll see you in the morning."

Ash was leaning against the wall in the hallway, waiting for him as he closed the bedroom door. "I'm glad I didn't promise him the extra book would be a long one."

"Yeah. I hear you. You want to… go watch a movie in the man cave? Or—" *Up here? In the bedroom?* Sammy would be asleep soon.

Ash stuck his hands in his pockets and squinted at him. "In the man cave?"

"I have a television up here…" It was nice.

And private.

With a locking door…

Ash pushed off the wall and into his space. "I'm sure it's very nice."

"It is. Wanna see?" He backed his way down the hallway.

"Mhm." Ash held his gaze, following him—*stalking him?* —right through his bedroom door. "Not too forward?"

"Nope. Lock the door behind you." He waited until that was done, then flipped Ash and pressed him against the door, slamming their lips together.

Ash grunted, right there with him, matching his energy. Ash tasted like need as he opened and let Bastian's tongue in, fingers sliding into his hair. They fed off each other, both of them moaning and rubbing together like they wanted to catch fire.

Ash's hands dropped to his waist and untucked his shirt, pushing it up with hot fingers that felt as if they might sear his skin. "Fucking abs. Jesus."

He flexed, imagining that he was massaging Ash's fingertips with his belly. "Like your touch."

"There's more where that came from." Ash pushed his

shirt up higher until he could tug it off himself, and those hands explored his chest, tracing the muscle, teasing his nipples as they slid lower.

"Mmm... my turn." He grabbed the bottom of Ash's T-shirt and tugged, seeking skin.

Ash reached back and grabbed the fabric, pulling the shirt to dropping it on the floor. His skin was smooth and seemed very pale in comparison to Bastian's permanent tan. "All yours."

He dragged one finger from the hollow of Ash's throat, all the way down to that sweet little indented bellybutton.

Ash swallowed hard and licked his lips, fingers working his own jeans open as he kicked off his sneakers.

"Oh, hell yes." He helped Ash work his jeans down and off, then unfastened his own belt, leaving himself in his boxer briefs.

Ash kissed him again and those hands went right for his ass, pulling their hips together. They stumbled a bit before finding their balance and a sweet little rocking rhythm that had them both moaning. They were both so hard diamonds couldn't scratch them, and Bastian's entire focus was on those places their skin dragged together.

"You're making me feel like a horny teenager." Ash was breathless, fingers clinging to his shoulders.

"Nothing wrong with that, is there." It wasn't a question. He was more than ready to feel something that wasn't harsh.

"No." Ash pushed his briefs down low on his hips and caught his cock in a hot palm. "You're just really fucking sexy."

"Uh-huh..." Oh Jesus, help him. That was perfect. His hands opened and closed, and he figured out he had Ash's ass in his hands. Yum.

Ash moved those fingers from root to tip, then lowered

his own briefs and lined up their cocks before grabbing his ass again. "Better."

"Uh-huh. You're like a brand. Fucking amazing." And long and fine, just like Ash. He approved.

Ash rocked into him, fingers digging into his ass, and that cock gliding along his. "Fuck. I've been half-hard thinking about you all day."

"Yeah. I been dreaming things... lots of things, honey." He couldn't stop panting, couldn't stop his eyes rolling.

Ash took a step, pulling on him until Ash's back hit the wall, giving them much more leverage. This time when Ash rocked toward him, he could push back harder. That earned him a groan. "Yeah."

"Better." He got one thigh in between Ash's legs, giving Ash more pressure.

"Fu-uck." Ash started to shout but dropped quickly to a whisper, hips still moving, taking what he offered. "Good."

"Uh-huh..." He deepened the kiss, his cock beginning to drip.

Ash hooked an ankle around his thigh, closing any space left between them, and the kiss grew biting, teeth pinching his lips.

Jesus, his world spun a little and his balls drew up tight. He wasn't going to last. Not a bit.

"We're just.... I mean this time we'll just... better next time, right?" Ash was starting to tremble against him, and that pale skin was flushed from his nipples up.

"Take... take the edge off. I can't wait. Need this." There. Words. Good.

Ash nodded, and that was that. They humped and rocked until they were both sweating. Ash stuffed a fist in his mouth and grunted, and a second later, hot spunk soaked his belly.

That was all she wrote. His eyes crossed, and he shot, his entire body jerking with pleasure.

"Holy fuck." Ash was winded, head leaning back against the wall.

"Yessir." He was awful busy communing with heaven.

Ash lifted his head and smiled at him. "Damn. I needed that. So much need I couldn't think."

"Right. I can breathe again. Damn. Come on, we'll clean up and... do it again." He led Ash to his big old bathroom so that they could wash.

Ash hung close, hands never leaving him except to wash up. They slid over his back, rested on his shoulder, combed through his hair... just constantly touching him.

He found himself leaning in, moving toward Ash. His skin was on fire, and he wanted to pull Ash into his bed, explore every inch of Ash's skin.

They got cleaned up, and Ash pulled his T-shirt back on. "We should check on Sammy and tuck her in."

"I will. You can just chill. There's a minifridge up here, if you want water, Coke, or beer."

"A fridge in the bedroom. I love it. I definitely worked up a thirst." Ash headed for the fridge. "Grab my pjs when you come back? They're on my bed."

"No problem." He threw on his pajama pants, then peeked in on Sammy. She was out like a light, her book on her chest. He carefully put the book on her bedside table, covered her up and turned off the lamp. Then he closed the door before tiptoeing across the way to grab Ash's pjs.

When he got back to the bedroom, Ash had opened up a beer and was propped on pillows, watching TV. Ash set his beer down and smiled at him. "All tucked in?"

"Sound asleep. She was reading." He thought her day had just been so huge that she'd given up the ghost.

"She was so happy. I remember loving new school supplies too. Congratulations, Uncle Bas. You did it."

"I'm not dumb enough to believe it's fixed, but we're progressing. That's what I needed."

"Two steps forward and one back is progress. And parenting."

He chuckled, because no one—no one—would have ever pegged him as a dad. Or an on-hand uncle. He was just the cowboy that ran the ranch, made the money.

Ash hopped up and took his pajamas. "I figured I'd better have something on in case the kids call."

"Right? You want to snuggle with the TV on, maybe... snuggle actively."

Ash straightened his T-shirt. "Active snuggling? Is this a cowboy thing?"

"Totally." He had no fucking idea. It just sounded cool and like one hell of an excuse to keep touching.

"Well, okay then." Ash pulled him into bed. "Are we going to freak Sammy out if she comes knocking? Does she even knock?"

"She doesn't come looking. She screams. We're more likely to have twins crawl in." They were hard-core little furnaces.

"Well, they're less likely to ask questions. They share all the time." Ash chuckled.

"Mmhmm. They do." He might like to share some with Ash...

"Mhm." Ash slid a hand under his shirt and leaned in for a kiss. "Is a kiss active snuggling?"

"Absolutely." He took a soft buss, then another one. "Kissing is *so* active snuggling."

He could feel the smile against his lips. "You know that whole take-it-slow thing? I think we're failing a little."

"Shh… I won't tell if you don't." God knew, no one had a clue how much time they had.

Ash's kiss was curious, exploring his lips, tongue slipping along his for a taste. He opened up, soaring in a bone-deep way.

Lord, this was fine. He could feast on Ash for hours.

"Tio? Walt had an accident." Will pushed the door open and came wandering in, a stuffed taco under one arm and rubbing his eyes.

"Uh-oh." Dammit. Thank God for rubber sheets and washing machines. "Do you need to go potty?"

Will shook his head no. The poor kid was half asleep.

"Did you get wet?" Ash slid out of bed and started checking Will over.

"I don't think so."

Walt started crying from the other room.

"Coming, baby boy. No crying. It's okay."

"Tio! I wet! I sorry!"

"For what, buddy?" He wasn't stressing this shit. They were little. Accidents happened.

Walt was still half asleep and whining as Bastian got him undressed and into the bathroom.

Ash stuck his head in. "I'll get the sheets. Will is tucked into your bed, he didn't want to go to his room by himself."

"Want to go too!" Walt started sobbing, and then Sammy's door opened.

"What's wrong with the baby?" she asked.

"Not a baby!" Walt screamed.

"Whoa, buddy. Hey. Hey, it's okay. He had an accident, Sammy. No big."

"Ah. 'kay. Can I go get a glass of milk? My tummy is empty." Sammy was mostly still asleep.

"Sure. You want me to get it?"

"Milk?" Will's little voice sounded from the bedroom. "Choccy milk?"

"Sammy, how about you go with Will while Uncle Bas finishes giving Walt a quick bath, and I'll get everyone some milk. Walt, chocolate or plain?" Ash seemed to take it all in stride.

"Chocolate!" Sammy said, and Walt nodded.

"Sounds good. Chocolate milk for all." He finished getting Walt cleaned up and redressed. "Come on, and let's snuggle, okay?"

"Sorry."

He scooped Walt up and started for the bedroom. "Shh... I love you. It was an accident. No big."

Ash came back after a bit with three covered cups with straws. He had both very sleepy boys in his lap, and Sammy was sitting up next to him.

"Chocolate milk," Ash said softly, handing one to Sammy first. "Are they even awake?"

"Choccy?" Will murmured, while Walt just snuggled in.

"Sort of?" It made his heart ache, how cute they were.

"Okay. Um..." Ash set the chocolate milks on his nightstand and climbed into bed on the other side of Sammy. "Okay, hand me a kid."

He figured Will could help at least, so he chose that twin to pass over. Walt was out, snoring like a teeny tiny freight train.

Ash took Will and Sammy grabbed Will's milk for him, and suddenly, everyone in the house was in one bed.

His bed.

He was in some weird, wonderful dream, and...

And they were all in his bed like family.

13

Ash walked alongside Bastian on the sidewalk, trying to figure out how Sammy was really doing as she led them toward the school.

She was fine when she got up, a little too nervous to do more than pick at breakfast, and she'd been quiet on the drive. Now that she was here, she was almost stubbornly confident, walking ahead of them, carrying her books on her own.

Which hadn't stopped her from insisting that they both walk her to the school doors.

The twins were with Anna, so Ash and Bastian could both give Sammy their full attention.

Bastian looked handsome in a white button-down and starched jeans, his felt hat and bolo tie. It was the first time he'd seen Bastian really dressed since he'd arrived, and the cowboy cleaned up very well.

He hadn't thought to dress up until last night when Sammy asked him what he was wearing for the first day of school. He'd very quickly found some khakis, a blue button-down, and a casual tie.

She seemed satisfied.

At least there hadn't been any tears.

"I don't want you to kiss me, Uncle, but you can hug me and tell me to have a good day."

Bastian nodded, lips not even twitching. "Yes, ma'am."

Maybe he'd get a handshake.

Just like Bastian, he was more than happy to let this be her show.

"Okay. Because I don't want to cry, and if you're too nice to me, I might."

"I understand. I'll be cool as a cucumber."

That was pretty self-aware for an eight-year-old, but then Sammy had been through more than any girl her age should have to.

"You're going to have an amazing day, Sammy. I can't wait to hear all about it."

"Uh-huh. I'm... I'm..."

Bastian interrupted the upcoming panic. "Cool as a cucumber, right? Icy."

She lifted her chin. "That's right. Icy."

"Icy." He nodded. "You got this."

She stopped a few feet from the doors. "This is it."

"Have a great day. We'll go for pizza after. Cool?"

"Yeah." Bastian leaned down and hugged her. "Kick ass today."

Ash gave her a wink. "What he said. And you have a great day too."

Sammy took a deep breath, smiled at them both, and went through the doors into school.

He wanted to take Bastian's hand and kiss him. He wanted to cheer. And part of him was nervous as hell for her. "She's going to be just fine."

"Yeah. I'm going to stay in town for an hour or so. Just in case."

He knew Bastian was anxious, but the cowboy had done a good job of hiding it from Sammy. "Of course. You want to take a drive? Show me around?"

"Sure. Want to stop at the Flying Tortilla for breakfast? I want the chilaquiles."

"Whatever those are, I am in." His fingers were still itching to touch, and it was all he could do to keep a respectable distance between them on the way back to the truck. Bastian smelled every bit as good as he looked.

"Eggs, chile, fried tortilla strips. All the good things." Bastian winked over, eyes dancing. "Maybe most of the good things."

"Most." He chuckled, feeling himself blush as he added, "You're really handsome all cleaned up."

"Thank you. I don't have a reason here at home, much. But I will for the Cattlemen's Convention and all, for sure."

He nodded and wondered how long it had been since the last time Bastian had been hit on. That was the most businesslike response to a compliment ever. "The Cattlemen's Convention?" he echoed, teasing. "Wow. That sounds so hot."

"Ha!" Bastian blushed but grinned like a Cheshire cat. "It's actually pretty fun. I'll take all of us—even Sammy and the boys when they're old enough. I have a good time, and I learn a ton about sustainability that I can share with my clients."

"It might be more testosterone than I can handle." Ash split off, heading for the passenger side of the truck. "I have so much to contend with already."

"Nah, you'll do fine. I have faith in you." Bastian slid into the driver's seat, reaching to stroke his thigh. "And you got plenty on your own."

He took a breath; that hand on his thigh was warm and heavy, and he curled his fingers around it, finally getting the touch he wanted. Some of it, anyway. "I was starting to wonder when you'd notice."

"The third or fourth day you were at the house. Once I got a second of sleep." Bastian lifted his hand, kissed it, and then their hands settled on his leg again. Bastian started the truck. "I hope she has a good day."

That surprised him. He'd noticed pretty much right away too, but he was... well, they hadn't known each other very well yet. They hadn't spent those long nights on the back porch or playing cards yet. That was when it had gotten tough to keep his hands to himself.

"I do too. She will. She's smart as hell, and the teachers will love her." He had this feeling that Sammy was way more interested in impressing adults than kids.

"I'm not worried about that, really. I want her to make friends—I want to hear her giggling in her room with another little girl."

"She will." It might take a little bit, but she would. It was easier when kids were young.

"I hope so. I want her to be happy, you know? I know that I'm not her folks, but I want the best for her."

Poor Bastian. Ash could see how much he wanted to just wish everything better. "You're parenting. It doesn't matter what your relation is. And it's never easy. I've watched this a lot. You're going to want things for her she's not going to get, and she's going to want things you'd rather she didn't. A lot of the job is hoping and following her lead."

"Yeah. I just... My brother wasn't one of my fans, and I worry that I'm going to fuck up."

"That's fair. And you might once in a while, but look where she is compared to when I got here. You're doing great."

"I think you're a huge part of this, Ash. I couldn't have done it without you. I wouldn't have wanted to."

He wasn't sure what to say to that. When he'd arrived, he was really just doing his job. Today, he was invested. It made him anxious if he thought about it too much. He was determined that the kids not get hurt again.

But deep down, he knew it was already too late for that. He cared about them, and they were bonding with him.

And he was falling for Bastian harder by the minute. "They're such great kids."

"They are." Bastian chuckled as he navigated through the city. "So much damn traffic."

Ash didn't crack up, but he wanted to. This wasn't traffic. This was... easy.

"I know, I hate it when there are two other trucks and one Tesla on the road." He rolled his eyes dramatically. "Oh my god. And now you're stuck at a red light!"

"There are at least... forty cars here. You wait until next summer when no one local can drive anywhere with the traffic."

"I'll handle it. I'm from New York." He winked at Bastian. "You do cowboy stuff, and I'll drive in traffic."

"Uh-huh. I can back a trailer through three pastures without hitting an arroyo. Can you?" Bastian was chuckling.

He leaned over the console and grinned at Bastian. "Would I know if I hit an arroyo?"

Bastian licked his lips. "You would totally know. You're a smart dog. You learn quick."

He stayed there long enough to tease, then sat straight in

his seat again, "I don't even know what an arroyo is. I better google."

"Sure you do. You know those big-assed natural ditches everywhere? Those are arroyos." Bastian wasn't even making fun of him.

"Everywhere... where?" He laughed. "I may need a field trip."

"I'll point them out on our way home. You've seen them, you just don't know you have." Bastian grinned at him. "I've been stuck in lots of them."

Ash wanted to kiss that smiling face. He leaned over the console again. "We should go get stuck in one now."

"I'd rather get stuck in the bedroom during naptime. A long naptime."

"You're going to make me sit in a restaurant and eat chilaquiles while trying to hide that I'm half-hard? Evil. My kind of evil, but evil all the same." Beautiful and evil.

Bastian's cheeks pinked, but he reached over, gently cupping his package for a brief second.

God, that touch made him gasp. He batted the hand away, not that he needed to because Bastian had pulled it back so quickly. "You needed proof? That's not fair."

"Nope. I just wanted to touch. I like the way your cock feels in my hand." Now that was totally unfair.

"Hm. I feel the same way about yours." He didn't grab, because the poor cowboy was driving, but he did tuck his fingers between Bastian's thighs.

"Oh." Bastian's muscles went rock hard. "Damn, babe."

Babe. Okay, that was new.

Good-new. It felt great.

"Mhm. Damn is right. Just wanted to share how I was feeling."

"I like when you share." Bastian glanced over at him, offered him a shy grin. "Never did this sort of thing before."

"Felt someone up in a car?" He knew what Bastian meant. He was just poking the bear. "Is it hard to find guys? Or just hard to be out around here?"

"It's not even that, really. Santa Fe is super open. I'm just busy. I have the ranch, the business, my folks. It's just been balls to the walls for years."

Ash doubted some of that. Not that things had been busy, the ranch was definitely a busy place. But he doubted that Bastian couldn't have found time for himself if he'd wanted to. He still had all of those things, plus the kids, and now a new... *thing*—relationship?—and he'd found the time. He'd even gotten out to his barn to create a little.

He gave Bastian's thigh a little squeeze. "I'm glad you have time now."

"Me too." And that was simple as you please. Me too.

He didn't know how he was going to sit through a meal, but it was probably best they be available if Sammy needed them. He thought about a nice cold glass of iced tea. Frosty cold glass. Icy.

"I swear, I'm going to have to park and take a couple deep breaths to be able to walk in without my jeans being too tight."

He shrugged, teasing. "You're the one that didn't want to go get stuck in an *arroyo* for an hour."

"Too many goatheads in tender places, babe."

"Ew." Those things were no joke. "I guess we're going to pretend we wouldn't rather be in bed?" It looked like a neat place. Maybe the food would be a distraction.

"Yeah. I want to stay close, and I want to take you to all my favorite places. We'll have to go to the Plaza Cafe at some point. It was my only job not at the ranch."

He loved that Bastian wanted to show him around. He could wrangle himself down to a low buzz. They could get what they both wanted later. "I love sightseeing and new places. I'm so in."

"Have you ever heard of the Loretto staircase?" They headed in and lucked into a seat, getting waters and menus before he had a chance to answer.

"Loretto?" He wasn't sure he needed the menu. He liked to order whatever Bastian had when they went to new-to-him places.

Always eat like a local.

"It's a chapel here. The nuns prayed for a carpenter to make the stairs to the choir loft, and a man came and made them and then left without getting paid. To this day, they don't know how they stay standing."

"What? Really? Is that for real?" Religion was one of those strange things he'd never understood.

"Yes. It's a true story. No one still has figured it out." Bastian didn't seem as if he was teasing.

"Are we going to see it? I'm a skeptic. I think I need to see this for myself."

Bastian blinked at him, then grinned. "Sure. It's... twenty minutes from here. There's a bunch to do over there, and Anna has the boys..."

"Anna does have the boys. We're on our own until we pick up Sammy, then she'll order us around until we get pizza."

"Then let's pretend we're tourists. There's a ton to see, and we can explore." Bastian's smile was radiant, young, excited.

"Sounds great. But I want to eat like a local. Order me whatever you're having." He was a fan of that smile, and how the idea of touring around his own stomping grounds made the cowboy so happy. This was going to be fun.

Maybe almost like a date.

"Then chilaquiles for both of us, Christmas, over medium eggs." Bastian beamed at him.

"Christmas." He had to chuckle. He loved it because it wasn't something he'd ever heard until he came here. "Man, I'm hungry."

"I hear you. So, I'm hoping we'll have time to stop and get a fancy coffee at some point. Or maybe a hot chocolate."

It was August.

It was not cocoa weather.

But that was adorable, and if Bastian wanted to, he'd drink it. "Memory lane? Seems like it's been a while since you wandered around."

"Too long, but we'll have fun. I grew up here, but it'll be amazing to see it with someone new."

It would be. Even if it meant drinking hot chocolate in August.

14

Bastian was having a ball.

Sure, he'd touristed a thousand folks around Santa Fe. Rodeo stars, country stars, oil barons, fuck all amount of clients and ranchers and 4-H kids who he was mentoring.

Nothing had been as fun as this.

They'd gone to the Loretto Chapel, listened to the recorded story of the carpenter who had come and performed his miracle. They'd hit the gift store, a dozen art galleries, an amazing chocolate shop, and a yarn store because his mama had called and found out where he was, so she'd put in her order that she'd come pick up this weekend.

Now they were drinking tiny cups of traditional Mexican chocolate, and he was watching Ash's head try to pop off his neck.

It was sorta fun.

"What is this chocolate magic? This is so good." Ash took another sip. "Mmm. When you said cocoa, I was thinking Hershey's and milk. Not... this amazing stuff."

"Right? It's a glorious thing." He took a sip, the burn of the chile making his toes curl. "Not sugary at all."

"No, and it's rich and dark and...wow." Ash took another sip, not afraid of the spice at all. "This has been such a... cool day."

"It has been amazing. I've had a ball. Thank you for letting me show you my hometown."

"We need to get out more often." Ash laughed. "I sound just like a parent. They never have time."

"No, but one day, both the twins will be in school too, and we'll be able to play." Listen to him, talking about years from now.

"One day." Ash didn't give him any push back on that at all. "I usually find something to keep me busy when the little ones are in school—laundry, cleaning—something. But I guess I'm putting down some roots in New Mexico, hm?"

"Are you interested in any animals of your own?" They lived on a ranch—the options were endless.

Ash blinked at him over his cup of chocolate. "I don't know. I hadn't thought about it. I'll be glad when Blossom joins the family; I love dogs. Anna told me I need a horse."

"We can do that. Do you want an older one you can ride straight away, or do you want a younger one you can raise up while you learn to ride on another mount?" He had a couple of six-month-old fillies and one colt Ash could choose from.

"Wow. I don't know. What's better? I want to learn to ride now, but it would be cool to learn how to raise one." Ash shrugged. "Kids, I know something about. Horses, not so much."

"So, go with option two. Raise one up, learn to ride on one of the older trail horses, so that when we break the other to ride, you're well-experienced." That was easy.

"Okay. Cool." Ash gave him a bright smile and set his chocolate down. "That was so good. Whoever invented spicy hot chocolate was brilliant. I had no idea there was such a thing."

"That would be the ancient Mayans." Bastian grinned and winked, only feeling a little bit like a shit.

"Ha. Funny." Ash snorted. "Hieroglyphs, the calendar, and chocolate. I can't wait until Sammy learns all about it. I see a field trip in our future."

"Oh, you know it. You ever been to Chichén Itzá? It's cool as all get out. I went to Mexico to see it with my best friend when I was seventeen." They'd had a ball.

"I've never been anywhere. I stayed home with the kids when the parents traveled. That's the job. That sounds really cool though. I've seen pictures, of course."

"No. No, that's not how it works." They all needed to go and see and do. That was how educated, tolerant people were created.

Ash leaned back in his seat, his tone teasing. "No? Even the rules are different in New Mexico?"

"I don't know about that, but I do know that they're different for the Martindale family. I won't leave you behind. I probably won't leave the kids behind."

"Where are we going?" Ash stood up and pushed his chair in. "Other than back to school to get your girl. Who did *not* call us today."

"I know! That's got to be a win, right?" He was over the moon, to be honest.

"Unless she's been sent to the principal for trying to teach the class. But I'm hopeful."

"This is one of those schools for smart kids. They're

probably used to that." He wasn't going to admit to it, but he'd graduated from a prep school, gone to college, had a graduate degree. No one needed to know that.

"Probably. Good call, sending her there." Ash gave him a flirty smile and held the door to the little shop for him. "After you, cowboy."

"Thank you, thank you." He headed out and led them to the truck, and maybe his boots were floating a couple inches above air.

Ash brushed by him, fingers ghosting over his ass before heading to the passenger side of his truck and climbing in. "Sammy's smart enough to figure us out, you know."

"I do. She's a bright girl. I won't lie to her. She deserves to hear the truth." He met Ash's eyes across the console. "What do you think about that?"

Ash swallowed and cleared his throat. "Well, I guess that depends on what you think the truth is."

"Fair enough." Bastian guessed one of them was going to have to be brave. "If she asks, I'm going to tell her that I'm having a relationship with you, and I want it to be deeper."

"That works." Ash was blushing right up to his ears. "I want that too."

"Then we're on the same page. I like that. Being on your page." His lips twitched, because that was so cool.

"I would never have believed I'd fall for a cowboy." Ash reached over and tangled their fingers. "I so need to get you alone."

"Yeah, we'll have to be patient, but I hear you. I want to take a shower with you. A good long one." But those boys would want Ash, and he'd bet Sammy had homework, and they had to share supper.

"I made it through the day, I can wait a few more hours."

Ash squeezed his fingers and then set his hand on the steering wheel. "Let's get the girl."

"I'm trying not to be all excited, but I am. I want her to have had a good day." He wanted her to have made friends. He wanted her to smile.

"She made it through the day. You might have to let that be enough for today."

"I know. I know." But he could hope. Just for a good start.

He headed for the school, telling himself not to chew on his bottom lip. It was one of his tells.

"I hope too," Ash said softly. "I do."

"I know. I know, but you're the expert here." He was the third-string starter in this situation, and he knew it.

Ash chuckled. "Pfft. There are no experts in this situation. None. And I'm a cold second to Uncle Bas, and that's how it should be."

"I don't know about that, but it isn't a competition for sure. Love isn't pie, right?" No one suffered from having more folks to care about.

"Nope, It's not. It's just made with a lot of different fillings." Ash leaned over and turned on the radio.

"There are a ton of pre-sets, but find what you like. You'll discover that the little miss is very into bubblegum pop." Him? He loved a lot of different things, even a little opera sometimes.

Ash landed on an alt-rock station that was also playing alt-country. "I listen to this one a lot."

"Yeah? What's your favorite all-time song?"

"All time? Hm... maybe... 'Radioactive' by Imagine Dragons. Remember that one? I was so into it."

"I do, yeah. I think mine was 'A Little More Country Than That' by Easton Corbin."

"Ooh. I don't know that one." Ash pulled out his phone.

"It's a silly little love song, but it always makes me smile, you know?" And he tended to like happy music. Unless he was sculpting. Then it was more... driving.

Ash turned the radio down and his phone volume up, playing the song through his phone speakers, nodding along and tapping one foot with the beat as they listened to the lyrics.

"Okay, I love that," Ash said as the song ended. "But I just have one question. What the heck is channel cat?"

"Catfish? Not a thing here." He did like to fish, though. "I'm more of a trout type. Do you like to fish?"

"I don't remember ever going fishing. My parents weren't into family vacations."

"No? I mean, I go fishing down the road in Jemez. There's a state park and all. What kind of things did you do?" Maybe the kids would like to go out there. See things.

When the boys were a little older.

"I read a lot. Rode my bike. I was into movies." Ash shrugged. "I played basketball."

"Yeah? You ought to put up a hoop. You can teach the boys."

"Hm. Maybe a junior one. They do have a one-on-one partner any time they want, don't they?" Ash sat up straighter as they pulled into the school parking lot. The place was busy, with lots of kids and cars and school busses.

"Okay. We get in line. You're going to bring the boys with you tomorrow?" Bastian asked.

"Sure. That's my job. You need to do yours. They must have a stroller somewhere in that pile of things you stored in the one spare bedroom."

"They do. I bet there's a pickup line where you don't even have to get out of the car. She might like that. I just... I don't know. You're on the pickup and drop-off list." God, the kids were all so short.

"I'll ask tonight after we hear everything she wants to tell us." Ash looked around. "Lines. Geez."

"I know. We just need to find her. There are so many munchkins." He felt like a giant, like he was old.

A small group of girls emerged from the school, all carrying backpacks. From where they were, it seemed like the girls were all talking at the same time. And there in the middle of the pack was Sammy, just as chatty as the rest of them. He pointed one finger, trying not to pull her attention. "Ash—look."

"Oh, dude." Ash beamed at him, at her, back at him. "Walk slower, Bast."

He nodded. Right. Slower.

Ash chuckled. "Gotta be cool, wait for her."

"Right. No making her seem uncool."

"Mhm."

"That's my family. I have to go, guys. I'll see you tomorrow." Sammy waved and walked toward them. "Hugs are okay. No kisses."

"Right on. How was your day?" Bastian grinned at her but didn't hug or kiss.

"Good. That was Marisa and Lucille and Penelope." Sammy shrugged, her grin more than a little tickled. "We're going to be friends. Penelope's having a pizza party for her birthday on Saturday. Can I go?"

"Sure. Just get all the details."

Fucking A.

Friends.

Party.

Go.

He wanted to just holler.

"We can go shopping for a present on Friday after I pick you up." Ash offered to carry her backpack and Sammy let him.

"Okay, cool. She likes Hello Kitty and stuffies. We should go to Target."

Bastian thought that they were going to hear those last five words a lot.

"Sounds like a plan to me. Target is one of my favorite places." Ash opened the door for her, and she climbed in, then took her backpack. "Are you ready for pizza?"

"Yeah. Yeah. Are we taking it back for the twins? I promised them I'd watch Paw Patrol with them tonight."

"You want to takeout and all eat together? That's fine. It's your day."

She nodded. "That would be nice of me, and I have math and reading to do."

"Already, huh?" Bastian shook his head. "Anything good on the reading?"

"*The Bookshop at the Back of Beyond.* I like it."

"Starting you right off, huh? What else did you do? Science? History?"

"Those are tomorrow and Thursday. We have art, STEM, library, music, and dance once a week. Dance. Can you believe it?"

"That sounds like fun. I bet you're a good dancer." They had promised each other some time together later, but however Ash was feeling, he was totally focused on Sammy right now.

"Yeah. I got a bunch of stuff I need before Wednesday. Can we go get it maybe? Like tomorrow?"

"Ah, the beginning of the year scramble for things they didn't tell us you needed before school started." Ash chuckled. "Every year. Every school. Everywhere."

"I remember that. I liked the whole searching for some weird book or particular pencil case." Bastian chuckled and shook his head. "You can order from Amazon, too, if you want."

"Ugh. Amazon. Boring." Ash rolled his eyes playfully.

"Don't make me beat you," he muttered under his breath. "Amazon is boring. Geez Louise."

Ash just kept giggling. "You have to shop for school stuff in person. Get your hands on things. Am I right, Sammy?"

"You are *so* right, Ash. How don't you know this, Uncle Bast?"

He shrugged. "Got me. Bad raising, I suppose. A cowboy thing."

"That's okay. Cowboys know all kinds of other very important things." Sammy nodded like she knew what she was talking about. "Without cowboys, we wouldn't have milk, and without milk we wouldn't have cheese, and without cheese, we wouldn't have pizza!"

"You know it! Priorities!" He wanted to hit his knees and praise God for this. He knew every day wouldn't be good, but this first one was important.

Ash laughed and seemed just as happy as he was.

They chatted and laughed all the way to the pizza place, all through ordering pizza, and all the way home. It might have been the most fun he'd had with Sammy since the day she'd arrived. She was certainly more animated and chatty than usual.

He didn't comment on it, because he wasn't going to screw it up. Please God, don't let him screw this up.

Sammy grabbed her bag and took his hand as they went up to the house. Ash followed them, carrying the pizza to the kitchen.

"Oh, boys! Who's hungry?" Ash called and he waited for the stampede of little boy feet on the stairs.

"Tio! Ash! Sisser!"

The cries were happy and loud, and Bastian's hands were full of sticky little boys. "Oh, my sobrinitos! I missed you today."

Anna shuffled into the kitchen more slowly, her eyes going right to Sammy. "Look who is home. How was your day?"

Sammy launched into her story.

Ash found plates and dished up pizza, cutting the big slices smaller for little boy hands.

It had been everything Bastian wanted. More than he'd expected.

They'd made it through day one.

15

Ash was finding it hard to focus as they tucked Sammy in. He'd been waiting all day to get Bastian alone, and while they managed a grope or a stolen kiss here and there, saying goodnight and closing Sammy's door couldn't have come fast enough.

The boys had been asleep for an hour already, and Sammy was tired in a way he hadn't seen her yet—worn out tired from a long day—and half asleep by the time they left the room.

Bastian glanced at him, and he nodded and followed the cowboy down the hall.

Bastian grabbed the baby monitor, locked the door behind him, and nodded toward the bathroom without a word.

He kicked off his sneakers and unbuttoned his shirt. He couldn't help grinning a little watching that silent cowboy's ass walk away.

Someone was in an amazing mood—and he was going to take full advantage of it.

He followed, letting go of a day's worth of telling his cock to take a powder. He wanted Bastian's touch so badly he could hardly think of anything else. He didn't break the silence though. There was something strangely magical about it, adding to the electric charge in the air between them.

Bastian started the water, and then he stripped down, baring himself and giving Ash an eyeful.

He admired frankly as he added his jeans, socks, and briefs to the pile of cowboy clothing, then breathed in the steamy air. He took a step closer to Bastian, reaching one hand out to touch.

Bastian dragged him into the hot spray, tugging their lips together. The kiss didn't start easy, either; it was hard and deep and hungry.

He pressed a hand against the tile for balance and caught one of Bastian's muscled biceps with the other, working to meet the cowboy's intensity as the water rained down and steam filled the shower around them. Bastian's cock pressed into his hip, and he leaned into it.

He felt Bastian's smile against his lips, the bare scrape of stubble against his chin. Every one of his nerves was lit up, and his body was on fire in the best possible way.

He smiled back, nipping at Bastian's lower lip, staring into those dark eyes. "Finally," he said, sliding his hand over to tease a little wet nipple.

"Uh-huh. Over and over. Ache for you." Bastian sat down on the seat in the shower, the water pouring down on him. Then Bastian dragged him onto his lap, taking another deep kiss.

He surprised himself with how much he wanted to melt into Bastian, just feel and let the cowboy drive. He'd never felt this way about anyone, and never trusted anyone else so completely either. Bastian was welcome to whatever he wanted, and Ash tried to let him know, opening and letting that tongue in deep enough to taste his tonsils.

Bastian's hands dragged along his spine, cupped his ass, squeezed and pulled him closer.

He scooted right in, arching to tease his cowboy's cock. Their kiss had grown wild, mixed with love bites and heavy moans.

"Want you." Bastian bit his bottom lip, just a little hard.

Ash nodded. He loved the shower; all the hot water and steam made the peaks and valleys of Bastian's muscled landscape even more beautiful. Maybe they could come back for the afterglow. "Yes. Fuck, yes. Please."

Bastian kissed him until he could barely breathe. "I don't want our first time to be a quickie in the shower. Come to bed?"

"Yeah." He panted and tried to focus. "Yes. It's a—a great bed."

"A great bed." Bastian nodded, dropping kisses over him, those hands still mapping him.

They couldn't get there if he didn't get up. He told his legs to move, and they didn't. He wasn't even sure how to wiggle his fucking toes right now, but after a second, he managed to slide back and get to his feet. Bastian groaned and reached for him, lips parted and hungry.

"Come on, cowboy." He took Bastian's hand and pulled him along, shutting off the water before backing out of the big shower.

He grabbed a towel and wrapped it around Bastian, then got one for himself. Bastian dried off like his ass was on fire before dragging him to the bed.

Ash had to laugh a little as they landed in bed, very happy to follow his cowboy's lead. He shifted up into the pillows, gaze holding Bastian's the whole time.

"Hey, you." Bastian slid up along his body, covering him completely, solid as a rock atop him.

"Hi." He barely had the breath for that one simple word. Bastian was stealing all his air. He reached between them and found Bastian's cock, curling his fingers around it.

Bastian stared into him. "I want to make love with you. You good with it?"

He stared back. Was he good with it? Ash started to say something flip, but then he realized that Bastian looked serious, and this might be a consent thing. How sweet and gentlemanly was that? "Yes. I want you too." After he made that very clear, he leaned up and nipped at Bastian's scratchy chin.

"I got slick and condoms. I was... I had hope." Bastian kissed the tip of his nose, then dug out a box of condoms and a good-sized bottle of lube. "A lot of hope."

He grinned at the bottle. "That is a lot of fucking hope. Do you need that much hope? Should I be worried?"

"Nope. Tickled. We're going to have a ball, you and me." Bastian winked at him, smiled. "A ball."

Bastian was everywhere—he couldn't see anything else. He gave the cowboy's hefty cock a firm squeeze. "We are."

"You know it." Bastian tossed him the rubbers and slicked those callused fingers. "You get to pick the next bottle."

"I bet I find a bigger one." He ripped one off the strip and tore it open. They were playing, but he was full of that first-time-with-a-new-guy nervous energy, even though he knew Bastian was into him.

Bastian was incredibly gentle with him, fingers stroking his hole without breaching him until he wanted to scream.

"Fuck. I'm not going to shatter, cowboy." He rocked against those fingers, needing more—asking for more.

"No? You're sure?" Two fingers pressed in, the glide stretching him and making him gasp.

He arched into the touch, his fingers digging into Bastian's shoulders. "Oh, God. If I do, it will be so fucking worth it."

Bastian chuckled and kept finger-fucking him, the rhythm steady and sure, making his eyes cross.

He lifted one knee and ran his foot down the length of Bastian's side, then bent it out to the side in what had to look like the neediest gesture ever and he didn't even care. He wanted this, and Bastian might as well know how much.

"Oh sweet Jesus, you're beautiful, I swear to God."

"I need you, Bast. Please." He moaned and tightened up around Bastian's fingers. He swore he could feel each knuckle. "Fuck."

"One more finger. Open the condom for me?" Bastian pulled out, slicked his fingers again.

He fumbled on the bed for the rubber he'd dropped and found it, already torn open. He waggled it at Bastian. "You want to... or me? I can—if you uh—Jesus." He already couldn't think straight.

"Uh-huh. I want." Bastian's fingers pushed in deep.

His toes curled, and he groaned out of sheer frustration. "Deeper. Fuck." Fingers were nowhere near deep enough.

"Condom. Need you. Come on."

"Right." Fuck. He reached between them, fingers trembling as he got the condom in place. "Okay. Okay. Fuck." He dropped back into the pillows and pulled his other knee up higher.

"Yeah. I need you. Now." The words were bit out, and they were punctuated by that heavy prick pushing at his hole.

"Oh, god." Fuck, Bastian felt so good already. He reached for Bastian's shoulders again, holding on.

"Mmm…" Bastian proved, in a matter of seconds, that he knew exactly how to make a man feel good, how to make him scream.

Ash rolled up against Bastian's thrusts, taking the cowboy's cock even deeper. "Oh, fuck yes."

"Yeah. Yeah, man. Need this. Us. You." Bastian slammed in farther, jostling him hard, deep inside.

He cried out as Bastian hit everything just right, then covered his mouth with a fist.

Kids. Fuck.

He was almost as hungry for that "us" as he was for his cowboy.

Bastian grabbed his leg, hips slapping hard against his ass, the sound ringing in his ears.

He couldn't get a breath; he couldn't keep a thought in his head besides how fucking close he was to shooting. His balls drew up, his gaze locked with Bastian's, and it was all but over. "Bast—"

"Uh-huh. Now. Now…" Bastian slammed in deep, his toes curling.

He shot like a spring had just let go, hips jerking out of control. His whole world narrowed down to that feeling and the man he was sharing it with.

Bastian was right with him, head thrown back, mouth open as he shot.

Fuck, that was beautiful. That cock pulsing inside him made him shiver and moan, but he couldn't look away. Bastian was as wild as any beast on his ranch.

They floated down, Bastian's breath easing, sweat making the hard body shine. "Damn, babe."

"Uh-huh. You were amazing." He puffed out a breath. "Driven. Jesus."

"That was—man, you make my eyes cross." Bastian slowly pulled away from him and rolled over, taking care of the condom and then slumping down onto the mattress next to him.

He liked how that felt, knowing that made Bastian a little wild too. "That was a hell of a cap on a pretty perfect day." School, their little sightseeing date, happy, tired kids, and smoking hot sex? "It doesn't get much better."

"You know it." Bastian's hand landed on his belly, solid and warm.

He sighed and curled in, resting his head on Bastian's shoulder. "Worth the all-day wait too."

"Mmhmm. It was a great day. I'm so glad you wanted to play."

"You're a good tour guide." He stretched, then snuggled in closer. "I have fallen pretty hard for you, cowboy."

"I hear you. You—you're something special, Ash. Important."

They were tip-toeing around the "L" word, and he wasn't sure why, but they'd both done it. It was a big word, a word you wanted to say when you knew you had no intention of ever taking it back. Still, it felt good to know he was important to someone on that level.

He inhaled Bastian's scent and closed his eyes. He knew they should probably put some clothes on—kids and all— and he'd get moving soon.

Not yet though.

This felt too good.

16

"Come on, baby girl! Go!"

Bastian squeezed with his heels and stretched out along Angel's neck, rejoicing as she flat-out ran, tearing across the desert.

It was early morning, and he hadn't felt like he could just go for a hard ride in months. This morning, he had slipped out of bed at five, left Ash a text, and gone for a ride.

It was chilly, crisp, and he felt so free.

Usually, he'd be up and working, but today, he let himself indulge.

It had only taken a couple of weeks to get into a new routine. He'd crawl out of bed early and get to work. Ash would text him when he got up, then get Sammy ready for school, pile sleepy twins into their car seats to drop Sammy off, then come home and start his day with the boys.

After that, things were more fluid. Pickup depended on things like the weather, how long the boys napped, and whether Sammy had something after school.

There was homework, dinner and family time, and the next day, they'd get up and do it all again.

This Saturday, there was a birthday party for one of the girls at school.

Jesus.

His eyes stung, and he told himself it was the dust, but it was part exhaustion, part sorrow for Stephen, and part terror because his parents were showing up sometime today.

He loved them both, but... he was fixin' to have to explain that he was thinking real damn serious about firing Ash and making an honest man out of him.

Maybe not this month. And maybe he ought to tell the man he was stupid in love...

But Ash was confusing. The man went about his day like he had a job to do—which, to be fair, Ash did—but then spent every night in his arms like they didn't have a care in the world.

Including his folks. Ash didn't seem at all concerned they were visiting. Not the least bit rattled about making a good impression or having to answer Momma's endless questions.

That was good, right? Surely it was good. It wasn't that Ash didn't care, didn't want to make a good impression.

The man simply knew he was amazing.

Angel tossed her head, letting him know she was aware that he wasn't paying attention.

She was right; they'd slowed down to a sleepy trot while his mind wandered away to Ash. If he wasn't careful, she'd dump him on his ass to make her point. She wanted to run.

"Sorry. Sorry, baby girl. I need to put my mind in the middle." He patted her neck and urged her to move, nudging her with his knees. He wasn't much of a reiner, and neither was Angel.

She kicked her heels playfully as she took off, running across the open land.

The wind took his worries and his good sense away. "That's it, sweetheart! Go!"

Angel ran hard, head held high in excitement instead of low and long as she was trained to do when she was working. The murky morning shadows got shorter and sharper as the sun came up and the sky turned a brilliant blue.

He pulled a canteen out as they wandered toward the house. He felt amazing, like a brand-new man.

Eric gave him a wave, loping in his direction. "Hey, boss. Thought you'd want to know your folks are here, and Ash ain't back yet. They're in the kitchen with Anna."

"Fuck. Okay. Okay, I'm going to get you to walk her out when we get back, okay? I was in my own head, and they're early."

"Can do." Eric walked alongside them, heading for the barn. "Anna's feeding them breakfast, so no bad there."

"True that." When they got to the fence, he dismounted and handed Eric the reins. "Extra sweet feed when she's cooled down. She ran hard."

"Yessir. Hey there, Angel, lady. Did you have a good run? Look at you all full of yourself. Come on." Eric led her off for a cooldown.

He headed in, finding a smile for his folks, because he did like spending time with them, seeing them.

"Hey, y'all! Oh, huevos rancheros? Smells so good." He went to wash his hands before he headed to get hugs.

"Son." Dad nodded to him, winked. "How's life?"

"Busy." And that was the truth. "Y'all?"

"Good. Where is the nanny?"

"Ash took the boys to the park after he dropped Sammy off at school." He thought. Probably.

"Good, good."

Mama reached up and brushed something off his shoulder, then straightened his shirt. "I was sorry we missed her; we thought maybe we'd get here early enough to take her to school today."

"Tomorrow, huh? And there's a birthday party with friends Saturday." And no, they weren't missing it for grandparents. Not this time.

"Oh, won't that be fun." Mama smiled at him.

"I thought we wanted to take the kids on Saturday."

Mama shot Dad a look. "She has a birthday party, Steve. We can offer another day."

"Sorry, Dad. This is important. She's making friends, and the counselor at school is very pleased with how she's adjusting, you know?" And he wasn't messing with that, dammit.

Dad sighed but didn't say anything else. He didn't need to. Bastian knew what the sigh meant.

"We are so happy for her." Mama stepped in before there could be any more conversation about the therapist. "And it sounds like you're doing so well with the kids. How are the boys?"

"Getting big. I can't believe it, you know? They're just— they're wild boys, but they're all love." He sat with his coffee. "How are y'all?"

They'd lost their son, after all. That was fucking brutal.

"Keeping busy." Mama sat with him. "You know."

"Your Mom has a bunch of friends now. I'm doing some fishing. I picked up my guitar again."

"Yeah? That's cool. I have good memories of that. I

bought Sammy a piano. She's quite the musician." He reached over and took his mama's hand.

She seemed to appreciate that and gave him a wink. "I have some ladies I walk with in the mornings, and we have excursions—shopping, movies, lunch. It's very nice."

"There's an envelope out on the hall table for you, son. Some estate inheritance documents for the kids, a couple of custody things that need your signature. Not a rush."

"Okay. Sure. I'm... I have to tell you guys something..."

He heard the SUV pull up to the house, just then.

Dammit.

Mama started to get up, and he knew she was excited to see the boys. "Can it wait, or..."

"Sure. Of course. Go see your grandboys." God, he'd wanted to tell them about him and Ash, but—

Argh.

Mama left the kitchen in a hurry, but Dad took his time, walking with him. "She was so excited she barely slept last night. That's the reason we're early. She got out of bed before dawn."

"Yeah. I know she's desperate to get to really know them." Bastian thought she wasn't sure what to do with a little girl.

Ash had taken a step back and was smiling as he watched Mama greet the boys. They hugged her and were both very busy talking at the same time. Then Ash looked up, their eyes met, and he got a wink and a smile.

He grinned back, because he owed his lover a blowjob for the free time to go riding this morning. They'd have to settle up tonight after everyone went to sleep.

Everyone.

"The boys want to show me their rooms," Mama said as she let them drag her up to the porch and into the house.

Ash followed with their jackets and a small bag of what looked like breakfast leftovers.

"Mr. Allen." Dad offered Ash a hand and Ash shook it.

"Mr. Martindale. It's great to have you here. The boys were so excited all the way home in the truck. I had to tell Sammy you wouldn't get here until school was out. She didn't want to miss a thing."

"Please, call me Steve. I'm glad she seems to be settling in."

"And you should call me Ash. Everyone does." Ash winked at him. "They're all settling in so well. They're great kids, and Bastian has been wonderful with them."

"Our Bastian is a solid citizen. I'm proud of him."

His dad's words made him blush.

Ash just smiled at him again and headed for the kitchen. "Did everyone get coffee?"

"We did. Anna made huevos ranchero too, if you want them." His body wanted to just follow Ash, not stay with his dad.

"Oh, fantastic. The boys didn't let me eat." Ash took advantage of the few minutes without the kids and put a plate in the microwave.

"Did they have fun at the park? Did you have to put them on the baby leashes?" He used those things all the time.

"I don't use those at the park, I want them to run, and it's fairly safe. They are a godsend at something like the grocery store though."

"I don't think we put children on leashes when you were young, Bastian." He wasn't sure Dad approved, but he wasn't sure that mattered either.

"Ask Mama." He remembered his, quite clearly.

Dad rolled his eyes. "Okay, son. Maybe I have a poor memory."

"These two are double trouble, Steve. Trust me." Ash hummed, chewing happily. "How was the drive?"

"Long, but easy. Pretty views with the sun coming up."

"Sunup and sundown are my favorite times of day here. The view from the back porch? It's just stunning, and it seems like it's a different show every night. I guess we won't get to watch it as much now that it's getting earlier, we'll be putting the kids to bed in the middle of it."

"Yeah, but then in the winter, you'll watch it with them." Dad tried to smile. "They're happy, right?"

"The boys don't really remember Stephen, I don't think," he admitted. "And Sammy has good days and bad."

"Poor girl. Is school a good distraction?"

"It's—" Ash started to answer and then stopped himself. "Sorry, you were talking to Bastian."

"Nonsense. You're with the kids. You love them. You know."

Ash nodded. "It's been so good for her. I don't think we expected it to be *this* good. She has friends and interests and good grades. She's so smart."

"She's seeing a therapist, so I think that's going to help too. She has a lot of loss to cope with." And he wasn't going to be ashamed of that. There was a shit-ton of baggage.

Dad nodded, clearing his throat. "That's good. Stephen loved that little girl."

"I can see why." And obviously Stephen felt he was capable of raising the kids. That meant something, right?

"I don't think he understood you, son. But she will. If you raise her right, she will."

He shrugged. "What's to understand? I'm a cowboy, just like you."

Dad grinned at him. "He didn't much understand me either."

"No. He wanted... something not here, not us." He didn't get it, but he didn't have to.

"Tio!" The boys came running in and went right to him.

Mama followed right behind. "You did such a nice job on their rooms, Bastian. And that playroom is just perfect. How wonderful."

"Ash and Sammy did the lion's share of the decorating and work. They wanted it to be special." He was going to give Ash all the credit, even as he juggled twin hooligans.

Ash smiled. "We had so much fun. Sammy designed it and we shopped online and then got paint. She's a good little painter, never gets frustrated."

"Good deal. I'm sure interested in hearing about everything. Are you teaching the boys their ABCs and all?" Mama took up residence next to Ash, and Bastian handed Dad Will.

"Want to go see the puppies? They're working on house training, the three we have left."

Dad blinked at him. "Three."

"Which kid was I supposed to say no to?" Bastian rolled his eyes, but he couldn't stop smiling. "And mama will be coming in shortly. Sammy's promised her a bed in her room. We're going to be drowning in dogs."

"There are worse things." Dad nuzzled Will as Walt squealed.

"Mine PUPPIES! Tio, mine puppies!"

Ash laughed. "You'll learn quickly to spell P-U-P-P-I-E-S around Walt."

"P-P-P-P-S! Puppies!" Those little boy's eyes lit up, "Walt Puppies."

Better was the way Will rolled his eyes.

Mama started laughing. It was pure and happy, a laugh Bastian hadn't heard from her in some time. "Oh, Walt. You're too smart for all of us."

"I 'mart? Ash! I 'mart too?" Will was almost panicked.

"You are so smart, Will, buddy. We are so proud of you both." Ash didn't miss a beat. "Are you boys hungry? How about a snack?"

Both boys started wiggling to get down, both chanting, "Snack! Snack! Snack!"

"Lord have mercy." He put Walt down and watched him run to Ash.

"Cheese and apple slices, coming right up." Ash sat the boys at the table, letting them kneel in the chairs instead of using their booster seats.

"Nee-nut butt, pwease?"

Mama blinked. "Pardon me?"

"Peanut butter, Mama. Pea. Nut. Butter."

"Oh." Mama giggled opening a cabinet. "Yes, my dear boy. Peanut butter."

"Nee-nee Butt! Yay!"

Ash and he cheered right back, in unison. "Nee-nee Butt! Yay, buddy!"

Mama could not contain her giggles and finally handed him the peanut butter because she was holding onto the counter to keep from falling over.

"Good lord, it's a crazy house." Dad chuckled, which was pretty impressive. He didn't laugh a lot.

"It is." And it was silly and wild and utterly bonkers, but Bastian actually loved it.

"Oh my goodness. I needed that laugh." Mama scurried over to Walt and kissed his cheek, then gave one to Will too. "Wonderful, silly boys."

Ash cleaned up his breakfast and did a few dishes while

his parents played with the boys through their snack. "Did you have a plan for the day?"

"I thought maybe we could all go get Sammy from school, and then all have an early supper?" He gave his folks a quick glance. "They're tired, and this is hard. They'll need an easy, early night."

"Mm. I bet. That sounds good. Is Anna cooking? Or I can throw a lasagna in the oven while you guys hang out?"

"For lunch? We just finished our eggs. We'll just have a sandwich, yeah?" No reason to stress. Not today.

Ash laid a hand on his arm. "No, for dinner, ba— Bastian. You said you wanted an early dinner?" That hand disappeared quickly.

"We'll take them out in Santa Fe. Maybe the Plaza Cafe?" He set his lips. Was he playing this out this way? He didn't think so.

That wasn't him. That wasn't decent.

Pulling away meant shame and hiding, and he wasn't doing that. He was a fucking cowboy.

"Oh, that's a good idea. Sammy loves that place." Walt tossed a cracker and Ash shook his head. "Snack time's over. Why don't we get outside, walk a little, see the—the small, fluffy creatures that start with a P." Ash winked at him.

"I'd love that, but I got to do something first." He went to get Walt. "Y'all. I have news. Ash and I are a couple. I'm in love with him. We're going to go see the little dogs. Want to come with?"

The whole kitchen went silent.

Mama's head tilted and Dad looked confused.

"Hold up." Dad stood up. "Back up and say that again."

Ash gravitated to him quietly and took his arm.

"Ash and I—"

"Oh, Steve, you are not deaf or stupid."

"Well—"

"You heard what I heard. Bastian..." Mama threw her arms around his neck and kissed him.

He hugged her tight. He knew she loved him, but he'd needed this response, right now.

"Well, well. Welcome to the family, Ash."

"Thank you." Ash shook Dad's hand, and he could see Ash's cheeks were pink.

"I am so happy for you." Mama gave him a squeeze before letting go and looking at Ash. "Well, give Mama a hug."

"Okay." Ash laughed and hugged her. He was all smiles and it was adorable.

"Son." Dad gave him a nod and went in for a quick hug. "This is good news. Surprising news, but good news."

He understood that, but it was the truth. "It's new-ish, but serious. I'm sure."

"I don't believe you'd tell us unless you were sure. You've always been that way. So far, it's served you well."

Mama and Ash were chattering away, each of them holding a twin because the boys had insisted on hugs too.

"Does Sammy know?"

"We haven't said formally, but we haven't been stand-offish either."

"She seems like a girl that would want to be told." Dad nodded. He clearly had a soft spot for Sammy.

"Yeah. I'll talk to her today. She wouldn't appreciate being the last to know."

Dad gave him a smile. "Did you say something about little dogs?"

"Yes, sir. Come on..." He winked. "Who wants to see the puppies?"

The answer was absolutely, definitely a yes.

17

As they left the restaurant after dinner, Ash was thinking this was maybe the best day he'd had since the first day of school. Not because they hadn't had good days. They'd had many.

It was those words.

Give Mama a hug.

and

Welcome to the family, Ash.

Welcome to family. He'd felt like he and Bastian and the kids were starting to feel like a family, but something about those words, words from Bastian's parents, made it all sink in.

He felt like the luckiest man alive.

Sammy came to him, hooking her arm in his. "How do you like them? They're pretty nice, huh?"

He smiled at Sammy. "They're good people, I think. Don't you? I like them a lot."

"Yeah. I didn't know them much, but they were always nice. They sent presents and texts and stuff."

"It's good you get to know them now, right? You're lucky.

Grandparents are neat. I never knew any of mine." They had all passed away by the time he was old enough to understand grandparents.

"You didn't? Why not? Did your parents not like them?"

"No, no. I heard nice things about them. They died just after I was born, and I just never got a chance to know them."

"Oh. Oh, that sucks. Nobody should ever die. Ever. Only mean people."

"Word, sister." He held out his hand for a fist bump.

She fist-bumped with him, laughing hard. "I have to do a diorama for *The Lion, The Witch, and the Wardrobe* for reading class. Will you help me plan it out?"

"Oh, I would love to. I loved that book." How cool was that?

He opened the door for her so she could climb into the truck. It was nice having so many people around; he and Sammy got to talk without the boys interrupting.

"Yeah? It's a little sad when Aslan died, but when he comes back? That was so cool."

Some day, adult Sammy would look back at that and catch all the references to Christianity—like Jesus rising again—but for now, it was allowed to be just a cool book. "I like how all the animals can talk. I'd like to be able to do that. Talk to animals."

Her eyes went wide. "Can you imagine? Uncle Bas would be crazy jealous. He loves those horses and talks to them all the time."

"He does. He's teaching me to ride, did you know?" He helped get the boys into their car seats, and they just kept chatting.

"Uh-huh. Have you seen him go? He's not scared at all."

She shook her head, glancing at her grandfather. "He's not at all like my daddy, is he?"

"I never met your daddy, but it sounds like they were very different. That's not a bad thing, people just are who they are. But I think your uncle is a lot like your grandfather."

"Yeah. Grampa is a cowboy guy for sure. I think Walt is too."

Oh, Ash didn't think that was even a question. Walt was fascinated and eager for his rides with Tio, unlike Will, who was a little freaked.

"What about you? Are you a cowboy?" Ash winked at her, but it was a serious question.

"No. No, I don't think so. I don't... I don't ride the horses or anything."

That wasn't stopping him. He didn't think he'd ever call himself a cowboy, but he wanted to ride. "Well, not now you don't. But you could. I mean... I'm an adult and I'm learning. Would you want to?"

Sammy shot him a vulnerable glance, her face unsure. "I... a little bit. My friend Jenny pays to go learn how. She says she wishes she could see the horses whenever she wanted."

My friend Jenny. Sammy had friends. With names. Not just schoolmates.

He was surprised how proud he felt. Like dad-proud.

"Let's tell Uncle Bast you want to try it. If you like it, then you can keep going, and if you don't, you don't have to, right? And you know you can have friends over if you want to. I bet he'd take your friend on a tour of the barn if you asked him."

"You think so?"

Personally, Ash thought Bastian would move heaven and earth at Sammy's wish.

He nodded. "I do. He loves this place, he's happy to show it off to anybody. And he loves you, so..." Ash smiled at her.

"Yeah, I guess. Maybe she could come over next weekend. This weekend is Mari's birthday party."

"Yep. I'll talk to your uncle. Next weekend sounds good." They'd talked a lot of the way home, while everyone else around them was talking to each other and the boys were sacked out in their car seats.

"So, today was art class. We're learning about color theory. Did you know a red apple casts a green shadow?"

He might have heard that, but what fun was it to say so? "I didn't. That's cool. Do you know why?"

"Because they're on the opposite side of the color wheel, I guess?" She shrugged. "I don't know that Miz Olivera said why, just that it was that way."

"But you know all about the color wheel anyway, huh?"

"Oh, do you paint, Sammy?" Bastian's mom turned around in her seat. "I paint a little."

"I like to. It's fun to draw and stuff. What all do you paint?"

Oh, he was proud of Sammy. It would be so easy for her to shut down.

"Oh, anything. Landscapes mostly. Sometimes with people or dogs or deer. I think it's relaxing."

"You can draw a deer?"

"I can. I can show you, maybe tonight." Stella wanted to spend time with Sammy, so badly.

"Maybe. I have to read and do math, but I'm pretty fast."

"School is more important, honey. If not tonight, we have the whole weekend."

"We're going to have to get these boys in the tub," Ash

said as Bastian turned into the driveway. Waking them up was going to be fun too.

"I think I want to make an apple pie," Stella said, and Steve chuckled.

"I'm going to the barns. I'll be in after a few."

Bastian chuckled. "After the boys are asleep, he means."

Ash shook his head, grinning as he climbed out of the car. "Fair enough." He reached for Will, hauling the boy out of his car seat.

"No... No go..."

Bastian managed Walt without even waking the little boy up. Show off.

"We're home, buddy." He rubbed Will's back. He swore these boys were way heavier than when he'd arrived. Will was like a ton of lead in his arms.

"Home. Ni-night." Will curled in, farted, and started snoring.

He'd laugh, but he might wake Will up again. Maybe they could put them right in bed? Would they sleep all night? Sammy ran ahead to do her homework and he fell in next to Bastian. "It's been a big day."

"It has. We'll just give them a spit bath and make sure they pee. They'll crash. Granny and Grampa are exciting, huh?"

"You told them about us." They hadn't had a chance to talk about it yet. "Thank you."

"I'm not ashamed of loving you."

Whoa.

Whoa.

That was the L word.

This was more than a big day. It might have been the biggest day of his life.

He cut Bastian off before they went through the front

door and managed to kiss his cowboy around the twins. "I love you too. This is a lot though. I can't lie. It's a lot. But I like it."

"So long as you keep loving me, we'll figure it out. I have faith."

He didn't know what faith was, really, but he had hope, and for the first time ever, he felt like he was part of something bigger than himself. If that was faith, he was good.

"Come on. We'll put the boys in bed and hope for pie."

"Sounds good." He was going to fill the time in between with some dallying with his cowboy.

18

The boys were napping with Anna there, Sammy was at school, and Bastian had plans.

First, though, he was doing one of his favorite things on earth. He was riding with his lover.

The day was pleasant, the sun shining, and the horses were relaxed and ready to exercise.

Ash was not a natural rider, but he was determined, eager to learn, and absolutely willing to practice. It was an amazing way to spend time together.

He watched as Ash finished checking his tack, cinching up the saddle. Ash's boots were still very new, and his jeans were a little New York for riding, but Ash was excited and happy. "Okay, you. I think everything looks good. You want to check me?"

"I do." He went around Appleblossom, tightening here and straightening there.

"Okay." When he was done, Ash stood next to Appleblossom, took a breath, and got his narrow little butt up and into the saddle all by himself. "Whoo. I did it." Ash beamed at him, so pleased. "I did it."

"You did!" The first time Ash had launched himself all the way over. The guys had loved that. "Good job. Go ahead and ride her out. I'll be a minute behind."

"Right." Ash sat up a little and gave Appleblossom a little squeeze, and off they went out of the barn. He could hear Ash talking to her as they went. "There we go. Okay, girl. We've got this."

Ash was doing fine. A little nervous, sure, but getting more confident every day. Appleblossom knew it too, and she was happy for the exercise.

By the time he joined them, they were trotting slowly in a wide circle. The look of concentration on Ash's face was adorable. He got a quick wave and a smile as they trotted by.

Angel bobbed her head, and Bastian patted her neck. "I know, but soon, we'll all go for a run."

Ash pulled up next to him respectably. "Where are we headed today?"

"Let's go look at the fence out to the north. It's about fifteen minutes out and back, so we're not too far." He knew Ash worried about being too far from the boys.

"North. That sounds good."

He and Ash had had a hilarious conversation about which way was north out here, during which Ash explained that north meant uptown to a New Yorker. Ash had the mountains now—and the sun—and understood which way was north out here.

They wandered out, the sun shining down, the breeze just a little chilly.

"You intending to dress up for Halloween, honey?"

"Oh, you haven't spoken to Sammy about this yet, have you?" There was amusement in Ash's tone. "You're the Mad Hatter, I'm the Queen of Hearts, and the boys are Tweedle Dee and Tweedle Dum."

"Oh, there's a plan... I assume Mom is providing the costumes?" It sounded like her, top to bottom.

"I believe they are conspiring. Yes. I'm a little afraid, to be honest." Ash laughed, and Appleblossom picked up the pace. He was pretty sure Ash had actually given her a cue.

"She deserves a chance to be a little girl's granny, right? She is over the damn moon."

"She does." Ash looked back at him. "You know I adore her, right?"

"Mama? I do. She loves you too." In fact, Mama liked Ash more than she liked him.

"You think?" He could tell how much Ash wanted that to be true. He knew Ash didn't have a family anymore, and he was happy to share his.

"Of course I do. I told her my plans and everything."

Ash glanced at him, then slowed Appleblossom down, forcing him to go along with them. "You have plans?"

"I do. I'm going to fire you." He managed to say it with a straight face, even.

Ash laughed. "Shut up. Asshole."

"Well, I can't hire my fiancé, can I?"

"Whoa."

Appleblossom dutifully came to a stop, and Ash nearly went right over her head.

"Oh. Shit. I mean. Wait. What?"

No. No laughing. None. Zero. Zip.

"Well, I'm going to ask you to marry me, but I need to fire you first."

Ash grinned at him. "I quit."

"Oh." Nicely played. "Well, I don't have to have guilt now. Nice! I have a ring for you."

Ash swallowed hard. "I'm going to say yes, so you better be really sure, cowboy."

"I've never been more sure about anything." He pulled the ring out of his saddlebags, opened the box, exposing the ring that was inlaid with turquoise. "This is for you. I love you. Marry me?"

Ash stared at the ring, then caught his gaze, those blue eyes watery. "Can I get off this horse first?"

"You can. You want a bit of a break?" He swung himself down.

Ash joined him. "No. I just wanted to say yes on solid ground where I could kiss you." Ash tangled fingers in his shirt and leaned in for a kiss. "Yes."

"Mmm..." Thank God the horses were trained to ground tie. He tugged Ash closer, letting the kiss go deep.

Ash pressed against him, giving him everything in that kiss. It was hot and hungry. "I can't believe it," Ash whispered as they came up for air and held a hand out so he could slide the ring on. "How long have you... where did... it's gorgeous."

"It came in two weeks ago. I'm glad you like it."

"I love you, cowboy." Ash smiled at him. "I'm going to marry a cowboy. Me. Who would have believed it?"

"Cowboys are seductive as all get out." Bastian rubbed their noses together. "You're fine as frog hair, Ash."

"You're beautiful inside and out, and I'm proud to be yours." Ash nipped at his chin and grinned. "Did you tell anybody? Am I the last to know?"

"You are the first. I thought we could talk to the kids together." What if Ash had said no?

"Oh my god, the kids. I'm going to be a... step-uncle. Or something."

"I think Tio Ash is fine. Or, whatever they call you." Tios adoptivo was a mouthful.

"If they can make the switch. Ash is fine, really. I'm just excited that I get to stay. Raise them. We get to be a family."

"Officially. We've been a family for a while." He cupped Ash's cock, squeezing gently.

He'd been in love for a long time.

"Yes." Ash gasped and stared at him, then leaned into that touch, fingers digging into his chest.

"Have you ever shot out here in the desert, nothing but sun and sagebrush all around you?" This was incredibly fun.

"I'm a nanny—*was* a nanny. I only come behind a locked door that I've checked three times first."

"You want to break that cherry?" He took another good, hard kiss, working open his fiancé's belt.

Ash nodded enthusiastically, sounding breathless as he answered. "Oh, fuck, yes."

"Going to bless the land. Make yourself part of it." He got Ash's fly open.

"Bless the—" The sound Ash made was partly a laugh and partly a moan as Bastian fished that long, firm cock out of the denim. "Whatever you say. Whatever you want. Fuck, I want you."

"You got me. All of me." Bastian didn't care if Ash didn't get it yet. He would. When they joined their lives together, they were owned by this land.

Ash kissed him and leaned close, fingers fumbling for his fly.

"I got you. Gonna make you come so hard." He nibbled on Ash's bottom lip.

"Oh... fuck. Okay. I'll—shit, I'll owe you one." Ash grabbed his shoulders and held on.

"Yessir. Love this. I want you to feel for me." He dragged his thumb over the slit of that pretty, hard cock.

"Uh-huh. Feeling." Ash took in a shuddering breath. "Feeling pretty damn good, babe."

"Excellent." Bastian spun Ash around, supporting Ash against his chest, hand going back to work, lips against Ash's jaw.

Ash arched, offering his neck, one hand reaching up to clasp his nape. "Jesus. So hot."

"You are. Blistering." He kept stroking, dancing his fingers over Ash's shaft.

Ash went up on his toes, and his mouth dropped open in that way it did when he was close to shorting out. "Fuck, I—"

"Show me. I want to watch you shoot out here under the sun." He reached around with his other hand and rolled Ash's sac.

"Show—oh, fuck, Bast. Babe!" Ash grunted and shot, spilling his seed onto the earth that once was his but now would be theirs. Ash's fingers gripped his nape, kneading it as Ash gulped for air.

"So fucking pretty." Bastian kissed Ash's temple, still holding that flagging prick. "Love you."

"I love you. I love us." Ash leaned hard as his breath slowed. "Fiancé."

"Yes. Fiancé. Forever, you have my word." Bastian meant it, to the bone.

"Well, hopefully husband one day." Ash gave him a grin, then slipped away and buttoned up.

"Oh, ho. Listen to you." He was going to love watching post-orgasm Ash mount his horse.

"What, you want to be engaged forever?" Ash stepped close to him again. "When did you want to do this?"

"Do you want a huge do? Something here? In Santa Fe?

Maybe a destination wedding?" He didn't care. He wanted Ash happy.

"A huge do? I have one good friend. I don't care if we don't invite anyone. What do you want? Do your parents have an opinion? I don't know if we should go away... kids and all. School..."

"So we'll just let Sammy buy a pretty dress and have my folks come down. We can hire a photographer and a minister. That's easy." His mama wouldn't give a shit.

"I love it. I really do. I'll invite Max because he's been my friend for a long time, but I don't have anyone else, really." Ash leaned a hip into his groin. "Could we do it on the back porch at sundown? I love that sky."

"Absolutely. Did you want to do it in the spring after the snow's gone?" He swayed with Ash, the sun warm and bright like it was blessing them.

"That sounds good. I bet spring is beautiful. And spring is the time for weddings, right, my handsome cowboy?"

"It will be beautiful, and we'll have plenty of time to plan any details." His phone buzzed, and he glanced at it. "But right now, we have mustangs being delivered, so it's all hands on deck."

"Whoa, really? Like now, now?" Ash found Appleblossom's reins and picked them up. "Okay, so this goes back over her head... and then—oh." Ash chuckled as he lifted his leg to get his foot in the stirrup. "Damn."

"Here." He put one hand under Ash's butt. "I got you, babe."

"Yes, you do." Ash laughed. "You're the reason I'm a little tender climbing up here after christening the earth."

"At least you're loose, huh?" Oh, man. He was funny.

"I am. Are you?" Ash leaned that pretty ass into his hand.

"I'm hungry, but I'll get mine, I know." He squeezed before helping his lover mount.

"You will. All you want. After the mustangs and the children and your parents are in bed." Ash chuckled. "So... way later."

"I'm patient, don't worry." He swung up in the saddle, wiggling until he got settled.

"Not worried." Ash got moving, walking Appleblossom in a slow circle around him. "I can't wait to see the mustangs!"

"Me either. We're getting two herds, because we've got the room for it." He had two nice-sized herds that had joined, so they could run a few more.

"That is so amazing. Are they just going to run?"

"Yes. They're wild mustangs. We're going to let them be wild. We'll make sure the vets put eyes on them on the regular, we'll assure there is food and water available." The horses were his passion, and he would do a lot for them.

"How cool!" Ash was always eager to learn new things. "Do you need help? Let's ride, cowboy."

"You got it, lover. You want to try a little trot?"

"You got it." Ash seemed confident, and after a moment of confused signals, Appleblossom took up a nice trot.

"There you go." He watched Ash's butt, which was staying, for the most part, in the saddle. "Come on, girl. Let's catch up."

They did have to cowboy up, after all.

19

"**W**ow."

"I know, right?"

Ash stared out the back door, hand on Sammy's shoulders as they watched the snow come down. "That is not the same as snow up north."

"It's not. It's... fluffier." She tilted her head and frowned. "Why?"

"It's drier here. Up north the wetter air makes the snow heavier." Here it just flew around on the wind in all directions. "I think, anyway. I wonder if this will be snowman snow?"

"I hope so..." She frowned, looking worried. "Do... you think it'll be fun here, in the winter? Do they have ice skating?"

"I don't know. That's a question for your uncle. But I would think so, don't you? We'll make it fun. It's beautiful at least, right?"

"Can I ask you a question?" She was still looking out at the snow.

"You can ask me anything, cowgirl." He stepped around where he could see her face better. "Everything okay?"

"I'm worried about Thanksgiving. That it'll be weird. Awful."

Oh man. He'd known this talk was coming. He'd just assumed this was Bastian's gig. But Bastian wasn't in the house right now so...

He took a breath. "I get that. And I guess there's no way to totally make that go away, right? You want to remember and honor people you miss at the holidays. Maybe we can make some plans though. Something to look forward to."

"What if I don't get my favorite food? What if Uncle Bas doesn't watch the parade? What if he doesn't like Christmas?"

None of that was even a remote possibility. "He loves Christmas, and he's going to love it more with you and your brothers here. And what wet blanket doesn't watch the parade? We don't even have to get up early for it out here." The food thing was easy. All they needed to do was get a list and Bastian's mom would make it happen. "Will you make me a list of all your favorite holiday foods?"

"I—Yes. I like apple pie and mashed potatoes and rolls. I love homemade rolls."

"Oh... warm rolls and butter? Like the super-soft ones? So good." Carbs were the reason Christmas dinner existed.

"Yes... my momma made them with honey butter." Her eyes filled with tears. "I miss her. I can't remember her so well. Uncle Bas and Dr. Pam say that's normal."

He was not going to cry, he was going to keep it together for Sammy, even if this was breaking his heart. "I think they're right. I don't remember everything about my mom anymore either. But just thinking about her makes me smile anyway, so that's good. Missing her just means you loved her and that's good too."

"Yeah. Uncle Bas says that he'll have Granny send me all sorts of pictures, and that he'll have someone try to figure out the password of Momma's computer for those pictures too." She almost smiled. "He's not very good at computers."

"He's not." Ash chuckled. To be fair, he wasn't that great either. "You could make a neat photo book. I'll help if you want."

"Yeah? I'd like that. We'll have to keep it away from the babies. They ruin everything."

He detected no lies there. The boys were absolutely in their terrible threes.

"They are agents of destruction, for sure." One at that age was bad enough, but two? He might have thought twice about taking this job if he'd thought that through. "This can be just for you. The boys don't have to be included."

"Thanks. Can we... is there a way for them to have one? They don't remember them at *all*. Not at all. I mean, what will they do?"

They'd have him and Bastian, but that wasn't what Sammy wanted to hear.

"Oh, we can make copies of the book, sure. We could even give one to Granny. But really, you can help them learn all about your parents as they get older, right? You can tell them what you remember, talk about the pictures."

She nodded, lips twisting, then shrugged. "Do you think we can have a fire tonight? Maybe roast marshmallows?"

He was pretty sure he'd missed the mark. He'd have to talk to Bast. "That sounds like a great idea."

"Yeah." She turned and hugged him, tight. "Love you, Uncle Ash."

Oh.

There was no stopping his emotion this time.

He hugged her back, long enough to make sure that the tears stayed mostly in his eyes and cleared his throat so he could answer her without sounding like a frog. "I love you too, Sammy."

He wasn't just the nanny anymore, and he felt that more every day. These kids were his to raise now. He didn't need paperwork to tell him that, all he needed was this hug.

She smiled at him, then went bouncing up to her room, undoubtedly to her paints and her pens.

"Whoo boy." Ash swiped at his eyes and looked back out at the snow. *Get it together, man.* The boys would be up from their nap soon. He should probably go check on them.

"Ash! Ash, they were in my room!" Sammy's scream was absolute fury.

Uh-oh.

"Coming!" He took the stairs two at a time and skidding into Sammy's room.

Her toys were scattered around, one of the china dolls painted all over with marker. Her bedspread and wall had been—decorated as well.

Good lord.

"Okay. Hang on." He hurried out again to see where the boys had gotten to and found them both passed out in Bastian's—in their bed. He went back to Sammy's room and picked up the doll. "Three is the worst. Is this washable marker? Can you tell what they got into? I'm so sorry, Sammy."

"They suck. I want a lock. An electrified one." Oh, Sammy was pissed.

He understood. This was her space, and she was particular about it. "Yeah, um. Locks are—we're not going to do a lock. But I'll keep them out of your room, okay? This is on me, kiddo. Can I go get a rag so we can see if this comes off?" It should. He was careful about markers. He'd learned that lesson a long time ago.

"Yeah. Please. That's Angelica. She's special."

"Angelica. Well, I need some water so... come on. We'll clean her up together." He took Sammy's hand. "Tell me about her."

"She was my mommy's when she was a little girl. Mommy named her after a character in a cartoon."

Shit, this marker had better come out.

"That's neat. She really is special." He wet a washcloth and tested a spot out of Sammy's line of vision.

The streak of dead blue smeared, which was a good sign.

He hoped.

He leaned against the counter and got to work, letting her watch as the marker slowly came off the doll's face. "This is... she's going to be fine soon. I will hand-wash her dress too, okay?" He looked at Sammy. "Are you okay?"

"No! I'm mad! Stupid boys." But it was a normal anger of a little girl with a reason to be mad.

He nodded and started to take the doll's dress off. "I think I'll put up some baby gates on their bedrooms." That would keep them from being interrupted at night. Not that they had been much. Even Sammy was sleeping better. She wasn't completely through with the night terrors, but she seemed to either fall back to sleep on her own now, or need little more than a hug and someone to sit with her until she did.

Baby steps. But things were better.

"Okay. Angelica is all clean. Did I miss anything?" He handed the doll back to Sammy.

She looked the doll over. "No. She looks good, but it's snowing, Uncle Ash! Can I have a towel for her? She's cold."

Oh, snap. Some nanny he was.

"Whoops!" He grabbed a fluffy hand towel. "I don't know what I was thinking."

"You were trying to clean her up. You have focus. We could tie bells to the boys like they're cats." She wrapped the doll up and started rocking it. "At least the puppies were at training."

Yeah, the dogs were outside in their amazing kennels with the dog trainer most of the day.

"Oh, that's a good idea. Bells." He could play that game. "Maybe a pressure alarm that goes off when they get out of bed."

"Maybe an alarm on my door when they open it! One that screams, 'Get out, bad babies!'"

"Right! Like those fire alarms that yell 'fire! fire!'" He grinned and played along. "Maybe you can teach Blossom to sit outside your door like a gatekeeper."

"Ooh... I can do that. Dear Blossom, bite the boys on the butt."

"She can pick them up like her puppies and move them back to their beds." Ash led Sammy back to her bedroom and started stripping the bed, hopeful that the washing machine would do the trick. "We need a sponge for that wall."

"From in here or the kitchen?"

He loved how eager she was to solve problems.

"I think there's one under the sink in the little bathroom. I guess we need a bucket though, so... let's try the kitchen." He scooped up all the laundry and left it in the hall to put in the wash.

"Laundry. Ew. I hate dirty laundries."

"Why?"

"It stinks."

"Truth, girlfriend." He laughed. "You know what really stinks? Little boy laundry."

"Boys stink. All boys." Like that was an incontrovertible fact.

"Facts. Even grown-up boys have stinky laundry. Cowboys have *especially* stinky laundry." He laughed because that was no lie. Bastian's laundry was all man, sweat, and animals.

"Yes. Horse and cow poopie stink." Her nose wrinkled.

"Ugh. The worst." He found a bucket and a sponge under the kitchen sink and put a couple of inches of water in the bucket. "We got this, yeah?"

"Yeah. Yeah, we got this. We so rock."

That was adorable.

They got the wall cleaned and the laundry going, then remade Sammy's bed with fresh sheets. "I wonder if you get snow days from school?"

"I do, yes. And I can do virtual work for extra credit or if we need time off. Cool, huh?"

"Virtual work. That's amazing." He would have loved that as a kid. He was not the best at socializing.

"Yeah. Not as cool as my friends, but pretty neat."

"Well, it's good for extra credit, I guess."

She nodded, so happy. "I've done a bunch. The teachers say I'm doing good and stuff."

"You're a smart girl, Sammy. Your uncle and I say it all the time." He sat on her freshly made bed. "So. The boys are waking up. I can hear them talking. I'm going to grab them before they get into trouble in your uncle's room too."

"It's your room too, isn't it?" Oh, clever girl.

He smiled at her. "It is. We haven't talked about that much, have we?"

"Nope. I know Uncle Bas is going to marry you in May. I

know he said that he's in love with you, and that you're not the nanny anymore." She stared at him. "I asked if we were getting another nanny."

He laughed and put an arm around her shoulders. "No. We're not. I'm just changing jobs to Uncle instead." He leaned toward her. "I'm in love with him too."

"Good. He wants to be our family. He wants us all to be together."

He smiled. He knew that was true. He'd never felt so welcome, so wanted, anywhere. "I know. That makes me super happy. How about you?"

She glanced at him, lips twisting as she fought her smile. "You're okay."

He snorted. "I'll do, huh?"

He herded the boys off the bed and back into their room. They shared a room now, a switch he'd made to make everyone's lives easier. Eventually they could each have their own again. For now, they shared everything anyway.

"See puppies, Unca?" Walt asked, wide-eyed and innocent. "Play with puppies?"

Unca. That felt just right. "You know it, buddy. Potty, snack, then puppies. Deal?"

"Uh-huh. Anpanamples?"

"Pineapple? I think we have some. Yes."

"I think the way he says that it harder to say than the real word," Sammy said, giggling.

He laughed and got the boys through the potty routine, then headed for the stairs.

The boys sang together as they stomped down the stairs, both of them purely joyous.

Then they saw the snow outside, and their eyes went wide.

"Snow, guys. Do you like snow?" He followed them to the windows in the foyer.

"Snow! Chis-mas!" Walt pressed his hands against the window and jumped up and down.

Will nodded. "Sanna! Ho-ho Man!"

They started jumping and bouncing, singing "Ho-ho Man! Ho-ho Man!"

Wow.

"Soon, but we have Halloween first." He wasn't sure why he bothered, there no hope either of them could hear him. He smiled, though, because those were some very happy little boys.

Sammy rolled her eyes, heading into the kitchen. "Can I have a Coke? Please?"

"Yes, you *may*." He rolled his eyes at himself. "Come on boys, snacks."

"Play?" Will begged.

"No. Anpanamples!" Walt shook his head.

"Snack first, Will. Then we can play." Like always, after nap. Routines were important with this age. "Do you want pineapples too?"

Will frowned. "No. Cheese!"

"I'm positive we have cheese. Come on, guys. Sister is in the kitchen waiting for us." One thing that was always in their fridge was cheese.

"Okay!" They ran off together. From the back, it was hard to tell them apart.

So, this was his life now. A sassy niece, snow, puppies, negotiations with polar opposite twins, and a hot cowboy.

And Christmas was coming.

He'd take it.

20

Mama and Dad were coming in for the holidays and Sammy's birthday. This was the kids' first Thanksgiving and Christmas without their parents, and Sammy's first birthday here. The snows had hit hard and early, and they were back with a vengeance. Bastian had a flock of churro sheep that someone had dumped, a sick mare, and then Wylie came in and announced that Anna was pregnant.

Good lord and butter.

Bastian grabbed himself a cup of coffee and went to stand at the patio door.

"Uh-oh. The cowboy is staring out the back door." Ash slipped an arm around his waist and kissed his shoulder.

"Hey, you. It's really coming down. I haven't seen this early a winter in a long time."

"I haven't seen this much snow... maybe ever. The kids love it though. Is this a problem for the ranch? The animals?"

"Mainly for us just wandering back and forth. We have wood for the fireplaces. We're good if we lose electricity."

Hell, Mama and Dad were driving in it. "Even Sammy can go in virtually."

"Okay, good. Then why so pensive? You know, you stress every time your parents are headed this way. They're good people. We've got this."

"Oh, just working out the next few—did I tell you Wyatt had news?" Had he even told Ash yet?

"No." Ash moved around to look at him. "Is it bad news?"

"No. Well, inconvenient news for a bit, but—" He couldn't stop his grin. He was so tickled for his friends. "She's pregnant. There's going to be a new baby around."

"Yeah? Oh wow. Good for her! Them. Good for them. We'll manage. We're lucky we have her at all." Ash grinned. "I better up my enchilada game. As in, I have zero enchilada game."

"We'll figure it. She's staying on. She'll take six weeks off, and then just take another twelve at part-time. There's no reason to have to put a little one in daycare."

"Of course not. Can't you just give her the time? You can afford to pay her. I'll pick up the slack. With Sammy in school, I can handle it. She should be home if she can be."

"Oh, she'll stay on the payroll." He wasn't going to make it harder. "I just meant that she'll bring the little one up here to the house when she's cooking."

That way he got to see the baby too.

"Your six-weeks and twelve-weeks sounded so... official. Like you're trying to run a business or something." Ash grinned at him.

"Oh, no. I was more in: we'll need to cook for ourselves for a month and a half, and I'll bring in a cleaning service for the house so she's not having to do that." In fact, that might not be a terrible long-term idea. Anna had them to feed, the cowboys. She could cook and manage the house.

"Why don't you make those decisions, Ash. You're in here. You'll have to deal with folks. We've got a household budget."

That would give Ash more involvement in the running of things, right?

"We, uh—wait. What?" Ash blinked at him.

"What what? You're damn suited to it, but if you want to do something else, you so can. We've got to get us a bank account and all. We take a salary off the business—that's outside the budgeting cost of running everything."

"No, it's fine. I just—I'm just a little slow here, catching up. I forgot I don't work here anymore." Ash shook his head, grinning. "I better earn my keep."

The words were teasing, and poor Ash really did seem completely blind-sided.

"I guess you better show me the budget."

"We'll have to sit down and go over the line-by-lines." Maybe he'd just have Henry go over them with Ash. So boring. "You'll have a salary—you think two thousand a week will be okay for just your personal expenses?"

Ash laughed. "Two grand? No, babe. A gas card so I can get Sammy to school and like fifty bucks should do it."

"Of course you can have the gas card, plus a card for household stuff, school stuff. This is just for you." Fifty bucks. No. This was his man.

He deserved everything.

"Okay. That works." Ash leaned on him. "You think though—you think I should have my own truck?"

"Of course. Do you know what you want? We can call the GMC dealership and have it ordered." Jack was a good guy and worked with them all the time.

"Oh, not huge, but big enough to haul the brood around in and whatever gear or art supplies they need."

Ash winked at him. "This is a very grown-up conversation."

"Nah... buying a new vehicle is fun, right? Have you looked at the Yukon Denali?" He grabbed Ash up, playing. "Or maybe we get you a ten-speed bicycle with a wagon."

"Perfect." Ash kissed him. "Don't spill your coffee on me, I'm so over the laundry."

He put his cup down. He was going to have to deal with the sheep, but first, he wanted to play a little.

"Better. Now you can manhandle me. Cowboy-handle me?" Ash kissed him again. "Feeling less pensive now?"

"I am. I'm hoping Sammy likes her birthday presents. I'm hoping Thanksgiving goes off without a hitch. I'm hoping the sheep are okay."

"You're worrying. There are a lot of firsts coming up this winter, and kids are a day-to-day thing. Kind of like the snow—you rarely get what you're expecting." Ash cupped his face, looked into his eyes. "Seriously. Worry about the sheep. They're more predictable."

"They are. I don't suppose you want to make churro sheep yarn?" He had to tease. He had a buyer for the wool, but he could just imagine Ash out there, washing and dealing with the wool.

Ash laughed. "That sounds like it's above my pay grade. Do you often get random sheep?"

"Weirdly enough, yes. I get a lot of random churro sheep. People get used to me having them."

"That's so weird. I guess it's one of many things I'm going to get used to."

"Ash? Unca! We're awake!"

Ash grinned and let him go. "Baby gate for the win."

"Are my boys awake? The puppies are in the mud room, waiting for you."

Ash came down with the boys a minute later, and they disappeared right into the mudroom. "They didn't even want snacks first."

"Well, Unca Ash. *Puppies.*" Bastian understood. His first word had been *horse.*

"Oh, I know. And they're almost as big as the boys now. How long before we call them dogs?"

"When they're breeding and there's a new set to be puppies?" That seemed to be how it worked, right?

Ash shook his head. "I better make them some breakfast. They're going to be hangry soon enough. Have you eaten?"

"I had coffee. Does that count?" He followed Ash into the kitchen.

"No. The boys want egg wraps. You in?" Ash looked around the kitchen and got out the eggs. "I guess Anna is... a little sick this morning?"

He winked at Ash. "A little..."

He'd gotten a blow-by-blow.

Ash chuckled. "Well, good thing I am capable of making eggs." Ash got to work. "I wonder if Sammy is sleeping in or hiding from her brothers?"

"She was down early asking for cocoa, but then she went back upstairs." She hadn't been grumpy, but she hadn't been social.

"Sounds like she wants some her-time." Ash toasted up the tortillas like a pro. He must have been learning from Anna. They might survive maternity leave after all.

"Yeah, she wasn't pissy or anything, so I figured she wanted some space." She was basically happy, and she was trying hard to be reasonable, so he was too. It was only fair.

"She's worried that we won't have all the food she likes at Thanksgiving, which is probably only the surface of it."

"Yeah. I know Mom wants her to help cook. They've

been Facetiming." That was the right thing, wasn't it? Surely it was.

"That's great. I think the more family we have around her and the more included she feels, the better."

"Yes. She wants to have a sleepover for her birthday. Is she too young?"

He hadn't been the world's biggest sleepover kid until he was a teenager.

"No." Ash laughed. "You might be too old, but she is not too young."

"I am totally too old. So, can you organize it? I mean... a girls' sleepover?"

He was not qualified.

Ash nodded. "I've got this. But don't think for one second that you're getting out of parenting the night of, cowboy."

Dammit.

He opened his eyes wide, fluttering his eyes. "Huh?"

"I will make the invitations. I will order the pizza and the cake and buy the party favors. I will set up the den with pillows and blankets and Disney movies and nail polish and popcorn. And I will take first shift. But 3 a.m. to whenever they want breakfast is all you, my friend."

Wow. Ash sounded serious.

"Listen to you! You sound like you have trauma. Have you been harmed by a slumber party? Do you have a trigger?"

"Ha! Keep that up and I'll give all of it back to you, and I'll take second shift instead." Ash assembled some decent egg wraps for the boys. "What do you want on yours?"

"Salsa, please. Do we send invites, or is it a she-just-tells-folks thing?"

"I'll ask her. I remember doing both. Make invitations,

hand them out in school. But I don't know what's allowed." Ash carried two plates to the table. "Sit, babe."

"Did you want me to get Frick and Frack out of their puppy pile?"

"Oh. Yes, I guess you should." Ash took a big bite of his breakfast, grinning as he chewed.

"Oh, Will and Walt! Boys! Are you hungry for some eggs?" He headed into the mudroom, snapping photos of two gloriously happy little boys covered in fuzzy dogs. "Oh, y'all are something else, aren't you?"

"Puppies!" Walt was as one-track minded as ever, but this time, one of the puppies hopped on him and knocked him right over. "Ow! Bad puppy!"

"Just an excited puppy, remember? Puppies are just babies. They don't mean to hurt."

Will came to him, and he took that little hand. "Come on. Let's wash up, boys."

Walt got up and petted the puppy on the head. "It's okay. You're excited. Okay!" Walt stuck his hand out too.

"That's right. Do you want chocolate milk?"

"Choco milk like sister, please!"

The boys held his hands and toddled along next to him. Neither of them seemed to have a worry in the world.

"On it, guys. Sit and eat your eggs," Ash called from the kitchen.

"Hanks first!" Will called. "Haveta warsh hanks!"

"That's right, buddy. You have to wash your hands." They were learning, thank God for favors large and small.

"Right. Good call, Will." Ash smiled at him.

The boys climbed up on the stool, and he helped them wash their hands.

Walt was quick—soap, squeeze, rinse, then run to eat.

Will liked to play with the water, suds his fingers up over and over.

Ash set Walt up with his breakfast. "You're not a surgeon, buddy. Rinse off and come eat, Will."

"What's ur-gone?"

"A doctor, buddy." He didn't bother to explain any more than that, and Will didn't ask.

No, he just dried his little hands on Bastian's shirt.

Ash chuckled and got Will settled with his egg wrap. "Are you procrastinating? Aren't you usually out there by now?"

"Have you seen the snow? I want to hang out here, have cocoa, and make snow angels! I don't want to worm sheep." Duh. It was wet and cold.

"Snow!" Walt bounced in his seat.

"You're the boss. I guess you can make everyone worm in the snow without you, huh?"

"Hrm... I—I guess I ought to take advantage of being the boss some days..." Why not? He hired folks for a reason, and it wasn't like Sammy was going in.

Ash got up with his plate but stopped and gave him a quick kiss. "I love it. Snowmen and cocoa it is."

"No-men?"

"Uh-huh. For Santa Claus to see. And snow angels. We should see if Sammy wants to play too." He texted the boys, saying he was going to stay home.

"Why don't you go tell her. I've got these guys." Ash put some sliced-up strawberries in front of the boys and started clearing the table.

"Sawberries!" the boys cheered, and he stomped up the stairs so she heard him.

"Hey, Sam. You want to have a snow day? Snow men and playing before hot chocolate and popcorn?"

"I guess so." Sammy sighed and closed her book.

"You don't have to. I just thought it would be fun to play hooky all together. No stress, huh?" He wasn't going to be pissy if she was hiding.

"Will Granny still be coming in the snow? We're supposed to cook tomorrow. Will we still be able to shop, or do we have everything already? I just want—" Sammy glanced at him and then shut her mouth.

"They are coming. They'll be here in time to play. And if we have to, we'll have one of the cowboys run into town, but we have a lot. Everything you and Granny requested, plus some extras." He leaned against the doorjamb. "You want to talk?"

Sammy shrugged. "I know it's not going to be like always, but—Mommy loved Thanksgiving. It was her favorite holiday."

"Yeah? Me too. I love the parade and the dog show. It makes me crazy happy. The food's good too, but I love that it's the whole beginning of the holidays."

Sammy seemed to perk up a little. "You watch the parade too? Ash said we could but... I didn't know if you'd watch with me."

"Oh, that's my favorite. I love the balloons, the bands, the dancers. That's where Santa comes in! The floats are so cool, too, and sometimes?" He paused for effect. "I watch to see if the lip-syncing is bad."

Sammy's eyes went wide. "Sometimes it's so bad."

"Right? It's like they're hearing a whole other song!" Oh good. Were they bonding? A little?

"Or they hide behind the mic like, you can't see my lips so you'll never know." She rolled her eyes. "And we all *totally* know."

"Yes. It's like... you're on TV, guys! We can see each eyelash!"

She giggled softly. "Or if they have a runny nose."

"The bands are cool too."

"Daddy liked the bands. He knew all the songs and he liked the marching."

"He was in marching band. He played the trombone. We have it, you know? His band hat too."

"You do?" She hesitated, like she wasn't sure she should ask the obvious question. "Can I see it sometime? Trombone looks hard."

"You so can. I was just saving it for you guys." He didn't need Stephen's things.

Sammy sobered a bit but didn't retreat at all. "Okay. Thank you."

"Sure. You hungry? There's eggs and all. I want to see if we can make a snow turkey."

Sammy glanced up again, grinning at him. "A snow *turkey*? I've never seen a snow turkey." She hopped up, dropping her book on the bed. "Eggs would be good. How about snow mashed potatoes? Snow apple pie?"

Fuck, yes. He was bonding! "Ooh... snow rolls and little teeny snow cranberries?"

"Snow cranberries could just be snowballs. Easy peasy." She skipped ahead of him and down the stairs. "We will have cocoa with the parade and snuggle on the big couch under a blanket, okay?"

"Yes. Marshmallows or whipped cream?" He met Ash's eyes, letting his joy show.

"Marshmallows for me, but you can have whatever you want."

Ash gave him a big smile and a wink followed by a supportive nod.

"Are you making eggs, Uncle Ash? Can I have one fried on toast?"

And just like that, Thanksgiving felt normal again.

21

The house smelled amazing, but Ash hadn't actually seen any of the food yet because Bastian's mom kept shooing him out of the kitchen.

He wandered off after his third offer to help and looked out the window at the snow on the ground and the blue sky, and the lopsided, partly melted snow-turkey in the front and smiled. The real thing was going to taste better, but it wasn't going to be nearly as awesome.

"Elmo!" Walt shouted from the den, and he headed that direction. "Elmo, Tio!"

"Yay Elmo!" That was Bastian, just as big a kid as the other three. "Do you see Big Bird? I love me some Big Bird! Gros oiseau, right, Sammy?"

"Tres bien."

"Big Bird isn't gross," he teased, giving Sammy's ponytail a light tug.

"He is learning French, Uncle Ash. He's slow, but he's doing it."

Bastian winked at him.

"Ah oui?" Ash sat on the floor and leaned up against

Bastian's legs so he didn't disrupt the very serious snuggle Bastian and Sammy had going on. He snuck a look at Bastian's dad, who had just glanced up at the parade and was shaking his head.

"Who is that girl singing?"

Ash shrugged. "Sammy? Any clue?"

"You mean lip-synching?" Sammy giggled.

"Badly?" Bastian said, and Sammy actually snorted. "Is she singing Rudolph or "I'll Be Home for Christmas?""

Sammy hooted. "Jungle Balls!"

"Ha!" Ash cracked up, snickering into Bastian's knee.

"Balls balls balls!" Walt and Will, who'd been dancing to the music, started singing at the top of their lungs.

Even Steve was chuckling softly.

"Boys! You're going to miss the dancing snowflakes!" Sammy waved her hands, seeming young and free and okay.

Not perfect, but okay.

"Snow?" Walt froze and stared at the TV. Will sighed and flopped into his lap.

"Hey, buddy. You like the parade?"

"Uh-huh."

"Do the snowflakes mean Santa is coming?" he asked Sammy.

"Santa is at the end, Uncle Ash." Oh, so dry, that eight going on forty.

"Oh. Yes. Of course." He leaned back and caught Bastian's gaze. The cowboy looked like he was in pure heaven.

"Happy Thanksgiving," Bastian mouthed. "Love you."

He blew Bastian a kiss and pointed to Walt who was climbing into Steve's lap. Steve lifted his book out of the way so Walt could get comfy and then went right back to reading.

It was weird to be sitting here with someone else doing all the work in the kitchen. He felt like he should be helping. He still felt like a nanny sometimes—not because he was treated that way, but because that was normal for him. That was what he was used to.

Sammy and Bastian were chatting, and it was amazing to see. He knew Bastian was desperate for a way to connect, but he hadn't seen how Sammy was searching for the same thing.

It was tough for them because Sammy was never going to be the cowboy Walt would be, or even Will. Sammy might learn to ride, but she was going to be a scientist or a doctor or an engineer—something brainy that would take her away from home. She might come back eventually, but what she needed wasn't here, so they had to work a little at finding common ground, and this was a great start.

The parade came to an end with Santa as Sammy had promised and everyone was on their feet cheering when Stella walked in. "Sammy, I need you for the mashed potatoes."

"Coming, Granny!" She bounced off, her eyes lit up.

Walt glanced toward the kitchen, and then Bastian said, "The show with puppies is next, buddy."

"Puppies?"

"That's right, my obsessed one."

"These two are like you and your brother when you were little," Steve said, as Walt slid off his lap again, eyes glued to the National Dog Show on TV.

"Lots of puppies!"

Will seemed perfectly happy to sit and watch the puppies from his perch on Ash's lap.

"So were they close as children?" Ash asked, and Steve nodded.

"They were thick as thieves, but Stephen needed out, and Sebastian is a cowboy to the bone. Hard words were said, and I didn't deal with it well."

Bastian rumbled. "You did fine, Dad."

Steve shook his head. "No. No, I should have tried harder to understand, and I should have pushed to be a part of his adult life, but I was mad and hurt. I felt like he didn't appreciate our way of life."

"He didn't."

Ash rubbed Bastian's calf. This was family business, and he wasn't sure what to say or whether he should say anything at all.

"I suppose. It was hard on your mother too. She always asked me what we did wrong."

"We didn't. We lived the life that has been ours for generations. There's no shame in that." Bastian's hurt was still palpable. "Different doesn't mean superior. He never got that."

"You're right, son. He never understood that. I wish he had." Steve took a big breath and puffed it out. "Gratitude is these kids, though, right?"

"Yes, sir. And they'll have all the choices they need, but this will always be home, when they wander back."

"Just like for you. Always your home, and now actually your home. And you've done such a good job with it." Steve's tone was warm. "I saw the mustangs as we drove in, and the sheep. Busy busy."

"You know it. I want you to see the new breeding stock too. They're solid and used to being handled."

Suddenly, the guys were talking livestock, the boys were focused on the television, and he was surrounded by family.

His phone vibrated in his pocket, and he pulled it out, already knowing who it was.

MAX

Happy Thanksgiving you turkey

He grinned at Max's text.

ASH

Happy Thanksgiving you overstuffed bird

MAX

The guys were just drooling over the pic you
sent of your fiancé

Oh, he could just picture that.

ASH

He's a hunk and he's all mine

MAX

I've put the date aside. Everyone is mad
that you're going small. They want you to
bring Bastian to New York.

ASH

Maybe. Might be tough with the kids

MAX

Think about it. Ask him.

ASH

I will

He leaned back and took a picture of the room with the
boys watching TV and the men talking shop and sent it.

MAX

You literally found the Marlboro Man. So.
Weird. Do you take the kids to school on a
horse?

He laughed.

ASH

Yep. I also chew tobacco and sleep with my spurs on. Idiot. How is the friendsgiving? Lots of guys?

He missed it a little, and his friends, but he wouldn't trade it for this. He'd wanted this his whole life, and it was better than he'd hoped it would be.

MAX

Good. We miss you.

He got a picture of the guys—the beer and the random pizza box with the rotisserie chicken and cheese ball and huge thing of mac and cheese.

ASH

Looks familiar. I'll send pics when Stella and Sammy let us see it. Have a slice of Thanksgiving pizza for me

Will had climbed out of his lap while he was texting, and he got up and joined Bastian on the couch. "I feel bad that your mom is all by herself."

"She's bonding with Sammy. Anna is here too." Bastian held up his phone. "She's been sending instructions and pictures."

"Anna is the best." Anna was teaching him how to cook some of Bastian's favorites, but also how to feed the masses, since he would be cooking for the cowboys while she was on leave. Fortunately, he'd learned that cowboys were more hungry than they were picky.

Still, in his first official act as head of household, a job it had never occurred to him would be his, he'd hired Anna's cousin part time for weekday dinners and to help stock the freezer.

Now he just had to get used to the rest of it. He had a budget, all he had to do was stay in it. No pressure.

Like, actually no pressure; the budget was huge.

He had a bank account for nothing—just for shit he wanted. He had a brand-new car. Anything he even mentioned that he wanted appeared on their bed or on the table like magic.

It was unreasonable.

He was being spoiled, really.

He didn't feel like he deserved it, but Bastian didn't listen to any of his more reasonable requests. The stubborn cowboy did exactly as he pleased.

It's not like he was going to complain. He loved the way Bastian took care of him.

"Uncle Bast!" Sammy came running in with a big smile on her face. "The sweet potatoes taste *just* like Mommy's!"

Ash had a lot to be grateful for this Thanksgiving and all of it was under one roof.

Their roof.

THE DAY HAD GONE PRETTY DAMN well, Bastian thought.

Sammy had had one little meltdown, and Dad had teared up during the prayer, but for the most part, it had worked out.

Now everyone was in their beds, and he brought a couple of mugs filled with spiked cocoa up to the bedroom. He needed a little adult time with his Ash.

"Hey, babe." Ash wandered out of the bathroom freshly showered, damp hair sticking out in every direction, wearing nothing but tighty-whities and a towel around his neck. "Ooh. Whatcha-got?"

"I brought spiked cocoa. I thought we could decompress, snuggle. Maybe make out a little."

"Snuggle. Make out. I like it. Couch?" Ash grabbed his robe and pointed to the love seat that sat in the corner of the room that they mostly threw clothes on, but they'd cleaned up for his parents' visit.

"Perfect." He loved their little seating area. "Want a fire?"

"That would be great. Want help?" Ash asked even though he had to know the answer would be no. Bastian was all caveman when it came to making fires. It made him crazy happy to make flames.

"I got it, honey. Bundle up with your cocoa." He handed one mug over and stole a kiss.

"Mm. Thank you." Ash took a sip and pulled his robe around him. "The cocoa is really good."

"Excellent. I almost got another piece of pie, but there is literally no room in my belly. None."

"God, no. I'm looking forward to pie for breakfast though. And turkey sandwiches for lunch." Ash chuckled. "And some online shopping. Santa's kicked things off after all."

"Lord yes." He got the fire started, standing to make sure it was going. "Do you know what we should get the boys?"

"Dog beds?" Ash grinned at him.

"Ha ha. You're hilarious." He was thinking a tent and sleeping bags.

"I have to keep you entertained." Ash patted the sofa for him to come sit. "I have no idea what to get almost four-year-old boys, especially ones who live here. Bicycles? Soccer balls? Ponies?"

He supposed he could get them both horses. That would be the easy way out and they weren't old enough to be responsible for them, and that was the whole point of owning your first horse. "We could get them tricycles too."

"Tricycles. That's a great idea." Ash held up his mug. "Cheers."

"Cheers, love." He drank deep, then licked the whipped cream off his upper lip.

"What should we get Sammy? How to build a rocket one-oh-one? Or maybe nothing so we can afford med school?"

"I was thinking art-y stuff. She does still like her dolls too. Maybe a neat dollhouse..." Girls were hard.

"Art stuff sounds perfect. Can't go wrong there. Maybe a table, like a drafting table to work at? One of those goose-neck lamps?"

"Oh, I like the idea of a drafting table for her birthday."

"Good. You better go into town and get one for her. I'm not sure we have time for shipping. She'll need a stool and a light, and maybe we should get her some nice paper too."

"I'll call into the art schoolteacher. She'll know where to go." He would get something here. No question.

"There you go. See? You're kicking ass at this parenting shit." Ash kissed his cheek.

"You think so? I think you're the natural. I just try to breathe a lot and not yell."

"That's the essence of parenting." Ash laughed happily.

"I want you on the paperwork for the kids, you know. They're ours to care for."

"The paperwork?" Ash turned on the couch to face him, looking as stunned as he sounded. "Your guardian paperwork?"

"Yes. We're going to get married, aren't we? They need both of us." That was simple as all get out.

"Oh." Ash leaned over and set his mug down on the little

table in front of the sofa. "I—wow." He heard the sniffle before he saw the tears and Ash swiped at his eyes. "Wow."

"Oh, honey. Are you okay?" He put his mug down, grabbing Ash's hands.

Ash nodded, squeezing his fingers. "Just a little—oh, man. It's just a lot, babe. It's big."

"Well, you're going to be here, and you're going to be Uncle Ash forever." He took a gentle kiss. "Not too big, right?"

"No." Ash gave him a watery smile. "It's good. It's all good." Ash kissed him this time, leaning into him hard.

He grabbed himself a double handful, deepening their kiss.

"Mm." Ash hummed and climbed over him, straddling his hip. "I don't know how I got this lucky."

"Blame Mama. She started this."

"Right. I need to say thank you." Ash shrugged the robe off his shoulders. This kiss was heated, and knowing fingers found their way to his belt.

"Oh…" Oh, he did like how Ash said thank you…

Ash got his belt open, then gave him a good solid rub through his denim before getting to work on his fly.

He stole himself another kiss, nibbling a little on Ash's bottom lip. Ash was focused, fingers busy pushing his jeans down low and working his cock free. "I can't wait to get a taste of this."

"Oh fuck, yes. Yes, lover." He leaned back and spread wide, panting already. Ash was a goddamn fantasy.

"Look at you. So handsome and hot." Ash drew a hot tongue along his jaw, then traveled lower, tasting and teasing along the way—sucking in one nipple, biting at his pecs, nuzzling his navel and even lower, kissing all the sensitive skin.

"Jesus, babe. You're making me ache, balls to bones." He stroked Ash's soft hair, the strands curling around his fingers.

"Oh? Should I stop?" Ash didn't stop, hot tongue circling the head of his stiff prick.

"No!" He whimpered, his balls drawing up tight. "Please, love. Don't stop."

"Mm. Don't worry, babe. I got you." His cock slid into Ash's hungry mouth and Ash's tongue scrubbed along his length.

He groaned, fingers curling against the sofa. The heat there was utter bliss, and it was all he could do not to buck up and take Ash hard.

"Mmm." Ash hummed around him and took him deep, fingers settling on his hips, letting him drive.

His lips parted and his balls drew up tight-tight. Nothing had ever felt as good as Ash—it didn't matter how Ash touched him.

Every touch was all he needed.

He rocked and Ash met him halfway, pushing his cock deep. Ash's fingers dug into his thighs, pulling slightly, encouraging him on.

His eyes rolled back, and he gave himself over to the pleasure, the pressure, the pure need.

Ash didn't rush him, but he didn't let up either, allowing him to ride the wave for a while. But when that tongue started driving through his slit over and over in between tight swallows, he knew he wasn't going to last.

"Gonna..." His eyes crossed, and he arched hard enough that he lifted them both up off the couch.

Ash shifted, hands scrambling for a second, but stuck with him until he relaxed back into the couch. "Mm. So hot." Ash looked up at him from the floor, lips swollen, face flushed.

"Sorry. Sorry, babe. You make me crazy."

"Bast, that was great." Ash climbed back up on the couch. "Are you good? I'm fine."

"Mmm... thought I'd jostled you." He pulled Ash right in close. "Hey, you."

Then he took a happy kiss, letting Ash melt him.

"You did. I like being jostled. Jostle all you like. We're good."

"Are we?" He pushed into Ash's robe, hunting that heavy prick. "Are we very good?"

"Oh," Ash looked down at his hands. "I could—I mean, I could be a little better."

"I think so..." He found his prize, squeezing the shaft, thumb rocking him.

"Uh-huh." Ash groaned heavily and bit his lip. "Fuck, yes."

"I love watching you fuck my hand. It's the most decadent sight." And it satisfied him, deep down.

"I—you—" Ash shook his head and puffed out a breath. His inability to find words would have been funny if this wasn't so damn hot.

"Uh-huh. You. Me. Us. I love you, babe." And he loved the lost expression in Ash's eyes.

Ash grunted and he knew his lover was close. "Bast—" Ash's fingers dug into his shoulder and that familiar grimace settled in.

"Come for me, babe." He slid the tip of his thumb through Ash's slit and that earned him a sharp cry.

"Fuck!" Ash shot as if he'd hit a button, arching into his hand, moaning through his climax.

Definitely forgetting to be quiet.

He was going to have to soundproof this room, but thank God for adobe.

"Jesus." Ash collapsed against him, breath coming in quick, light pants. "Love you, babe."

"Decent Thanksgiving?" It was for him, which he wouldn't have bet on six months ago.

Ash laughed gently. "Best Thanksgiving ever. *Ever*."

"Yeah. And it's just our first."

"They will all be this good because we are together, the kids are really adjusting well, and your parents are the kindest people on the planet." Ash took a quick kiss. "Next Thanksgiving, you can fuck me on the sofa. Next level post-turkey lovemaking."

He cracked up. "Oh. I do like a man with goals."

"The only goal I have right now is to see if we can make it to the bed."

Bastian stood and held out one hand. "Come on, honey. Up and into the covers."

Ash took his hand and stood, tucking one hand under his unzipped jeans and cupping his ass.

"Mmm... You'll make my knees weak."

"Good thing we're not going far." Ash caught him and kissed him. "I'm not going anywhere."

"No. You're home." He stared into Ash's pretty eyes. "You're right where you belong. Standing next to me."

22

There were ten little girls in the den watching *Wish*, two pizzas in the kitchen that had been pretty well demolished, and Bastian was saying goodnight to the boys.

Ash flopped on the couch in the living room. It wasn't a room they used much, but he needed to be on the ground floor with the girls, and he'd about had it with the kitchen. He probably should go check on the popcorn levels and make sure everyone had enough pillows, but he just couldn't haul his ass up.

Bastian's voice sounded, and he heard ten little girls crack up, the laughter filling the air.

Then he heard, "Uncle Bast! You're so goofy!"

Goofy wasn't a word he'd have used for the cowboy he'd met when he first arrived, but it fit now. Bastian was happy. Sometimes cautiously, but happy. And he'd seen plenty of goofy.

He managed to get off the couch and poked his head into the den.

Bastian was sitting in the middle of the girls, looking for all the world like he was meditating as he got a makeover.

Mascara.

Eye shadow.

Blush.

Nail polish.

Even hair gel with glitter.

"Oh. Look at you." He didn't even try to hide his laughter.

"We're making him pretty!"

"He brought us all this fun makeup."

"There's glitter!"

"This is the best party ever, Sammy!"

Sammy was beaming, surrounded by friends and carefully painting eyebrows on Bastian. "It's fun. Do you want a makeover too, Uncle Ash?"

"Sure. But first... who's got the lipstick?" The girls made room and he sat on the floor in front of Bastian.

"It's red!" One of the girls handed it to him.

"It's red," he repeated, looking into Bastian's mascara-lashed eyes. He waggled his eyebrows and opened the lipstick.

"It so is." Bastian pursed his lips, puckering up for him. "Washable, strawberry flavored, kid-friendly red."

"Delicious." He smoothed on the lipstick, which was really more of a lip gloss, and it sparkled like everything else on Bastian's face. "You're gorgeous—oh!" Someone was tugging on his hair, putting his wavy curls into tiny ponytails. "Goodie."

"Have you ever worn makeup?" Sammy asked, and Bastian nodded.

"I was in drama in high school and in college."

"You went to college?" That was another girl.

"I did."

Sammy blinked at him. "What did you study?"

"I have a bachelor's degree in fine arts and a master's in sculpture."

Ash blinked. That was... new information. He knew Bastian was talented, he'd seen him work. Somehow, Ash had just assumed Bast was self-taught or something.

"You're an actor?" Why hadn't this come up before?

And what the heck was Lizzy doing to his hair?

Bastian's eyes went wide. "An actor? No. No, I mean, I have, like in high school and college, but not professionally. Just for a class. You take a lot of different types of fine arts during your undergrad."

"You're full of surprises, cowboy. Also, your eyes are stunning under that shadow." He was only half kidding. The pink shade lightened up the dark brown.

"Isn't it pretty? I think you should wear more pink. I'm going to get my scarf!" Sammy ran off and Bastian chuckled softly.

"Mom was so right. This was a hit."

"Moms often are. Yours in particular. I wouldn't be here if not for her."

"Right? With a dozen ponytails. It's adorable."

He laughed. "So me."

Sammy came back with a couple of scarves and dressed them up.

"Oh, that's perfect. Liliana, you should do the blush." Sammy had never seemed so happy since Ash had known her.

Liliana turned his head. "Look at me, please."

"Absolutely." He leaned toward her. "Blush me, girl."

"Who is taking pictures, Sammy? You need pictures."

"Oh, hang on." Ash pulled out his phone, unlocked it, and handed it to Sammy.

"Oooh... selfies!" Suddenly the sound of pictures and

laughter filled the air. These girls were having the time of their lives.

Ash dramatically batted his eyelashes at Bastian. "Do you think I'm beautiful?"

"Absolutely. The rouge makes the look." Oh, Bast said that with a straight face.

"Your mascara is luscious." He leaned over and kissed Bastian's cheek, hoping that wasn't too scandalous for the girls.

"O.M.G. cute!" Sammy snapped a thousand pictures.

Ash couldn't believe that Mr. Cowboy had not only let the girls paint on him—he'd given them the tools.

He held his hand out for the phone and Sammy turned it over reluctantly. "You ladies need more snacks?"

"Uh-huh. Is there more chip and dip?"

"Sure. You girls come on to the kitchen, and we'll set you up."

They were a giggly bunch of girls, that was for sure. He wondered if they'd ever go to bed.

Then he wondered what he was thinking.

"Can we have Cokes too?"

Oh, God. No caffeine. "Sprite, ginger ale, water, juice?"

"Shirley Temples?" Bast dangled that like it wasn't Sprite and Grenadine.

"Yay!" The girls all lined up along the counter to watch Bastian make drinks.

"Thought you were leaving this whole birthday party thing to me," Ash teased, brushing past Bastian to get the Sprite.

"Like I'd do that to you. I love you." Bast winked one sparkly eyelid.

"Man, that's a good thing. Because since I'm staying up all night, you're on cleaning duty in the morning."

"I bet they crash. We'll nap on and off."

Thank God Bastian's mom had taken the kids.

"I hope so. But there's always one that can't sleep, or who needs to call her mom or gets lost on the way to the bathroom."

"Oh, yeah. I have everyone's number. It's wild. I'm praying for an easy night."

"Fingers crossed." He didn't think they'd get much sleep.

He put out chips and salsa and some cheese and cut fruit for the girls to snack on while Bastian made drinks.

Bastian made a lovely set of drinks, and they looked fancy enough to be from a bartender. "Ta-da!"

"Ooh!" The girls scooped up the drinks and spread out around the kitchen island, chatting and telling stories.

Ash pulled Bastian over to the kitchen table to sit down. "She's having a blast."

"Good. I need that for her right now, you know?" He could see the tension in Bastian if he looked close enough.

"Hey, she's okay, babe. Relax." He slid a hand over Bastian's knee. "She's okay."

"Shh... she's great. I hope her folks know that. That they see her."

He nodded. "They do, and that's all they'd want for her too. That's what we all want. Even Sammy."

"Yes. Please God, let us do it right."

He'd really thought that Bastian was past the worry—or at least that worry. "You have to stop putting so much pressure on yourself."

He got a sweet, wry expression. "I have to now, for my family."

"She's okay. Worry about other things now. Grades, soccer, whatever." Ash shook his head. "I can't take you seriously. You think we can wash this off now?"

"Girls, is it okay if we wash up now that there are pictures?"

"Sure, Uncle Bastian!"

"Thanks! Be back in a bit for the flashlight scavenger hunt."

"You're very organized for someone that claimed to have no idea what to do for this party."

"My mom had loads of ideas, but I remember flashlights being a huge hit when I was a kid."

He remembered that too. Everything was cooler if you had a flashlight. "My face is crying out for hot water."

"You look adorable, though. They... this stuff takes practice, huh?" Bastian waggled his eyebrows.

"They're in the more-is-better stage. When they're thirteen or fourteen, they'll go through the racoon-eyes stage, and then it will start to fall into perspective."

"Girls are hard, huh? So different than handing them a football and pushing them outside."

"Girls are tricky, but they are more mature and have more common sense, which boys... maybe never have? Boys learn everything the hard way but are good until they're halfway through high school and then they stop speaking in anything but grunts." He chuckled. "Of course, who knows with the twins?"

"They may never come down out of the trees." Bastian didn't seem terribly worried about that.

"Monkeys. Seems appropriate." They shuffled into their bathroom, which thankfully had two sinks, and he tossed Bastian a washcloth.

"Oh, I am a sight..." Bastian turned on the water and lathered up. "Wow."

He giggled all the way through washing his face. "I have photo evidence."

"My folks will have them printed." Bastian rinsed and dried off his face. "Did I get it all?"

"Oh." Bastian looked a little like a racoon. "No, babe. Mascara is like Velcro." He took Bastian's washcloth and went after the dark smudges under his fiancé's deep, dark eyes.

It was surprisingly intimate—not sexual, but close and quiet and something he knew belonged to him.

"There. All good. Me?" He batted his eyelashes.

"Yeah, babe. Close your eyes. You have glitter." Bastian's touch was soft as a feather, and it made him shiver a bit.

He smiled with his eyes closed and leaned toward Bastian. "Glitter will be all over everything for a week. Or maybe until Sammy goes to college. Tough call."

"It's weird and wonderful. I don't hate the idea, somehow." Bastian chuckled softly, and he loved that sound.

"You're such a good dad. I know you're really an uncle, but you're functionally a parent, and you're amazing at it."

"We."

"What?"

"We're functionally parents, Ash."

"Right." He always got all warm when he was reminded of that. "I wonder how long it will take me to start thinking that way. I've spent so long telling myself I'm not allowed to be that as a nanny, you know?"

"Yeah. Well, you're their parent, as much as I am. They're ours."

"They are. I know. I'm the luckiest man alive, babe, I'm telling you." He finally understood what the phrase "living the dream" meant, even if he still felt like he was actually dreaming. "To have all of this? I just can't believe it sometimes."

"God moves in mysterious ways. I'm just glad I have you."

There was a sudden shriek downstairs, followed by several more and the girls' voices carried through the house.

"Uh-oh." He dropped Bastian's towel in the sink and ran, with Bastian right behind him.

"Uncle Bast! Help!"

They ran in, and Ash gasped. That was the biggest moth he'd ever seen.

Ever.

It was easily the size of his hand.

"Kill it! Uncle Bast! Kill it!"

"Lord no. That's a black witch moth. Poor thing had to have gotten trapped inside, because it would have migrated away already."

Sammy stared at him, eyes wide. "No?"

"It's a moth, Sammy. It can't hurt you. Y'all go in the other room, and I'll take it out to the barn."

Maybe not, but the thing was huge. Cool. But huge.

"Come on, ladies. Let's get out of the way. Back to the den. Did you all get enough to eat?" He started herding the girls away from Bastian and the big bug.

"Is it going to bite him?"

"Is it going to fly in here?"

"Why is it so big?"

The questions flew fast and hard.

He was good at the rapid-fire answers. "Moths don't bite. Moths just look cool and fly around. But not in here because Uncle Bastian is taking it out to the barn where it will be happier. Usually, bugs get as big as they need to be to catch whatever it is they eat. It can't come back. The doors are closed because it's winter." He talked while he helped fluff pillows and sleeping bags. "Are you all getting sleepy? Or is it time for another movie?"

"We're not sleepy, but we could watch something and talk." Sammy slid into her sleeping bag, snuggling in.

"That sounds great." He handed Sammy the remote. "I'll come back in a bit and check on you, okay?"

"Okay, Uncle. Make sure Uncle Bastian is all right, yeah?"

"I will. Don't you worry about him. He's braver than both of us." It was cute how Sammy used "Uncle" like some kids said "Daddy." He loved it.

"Yeah. He's all rugged."

All rugged.

That was too cute.

"He is. No worries with him around." He gave her cheek a pat before carefully tiptoeing around the other girls as he left the room. "Enjoy your movie."

The chatter started as soon as he left the room. This was a good night, and Sammy deserved it.

They might crash during this movie.

Maybe.

Or maybe the flashlight scavenger hunt would happen.

He was up for anything.

23

Bastian stared at the Christmas tree, watching the lights flash.

Jesus, look at all those toys.

These babies were spoiled rotten. Just absolutely.

He'd feel worse if it wasn't so much fun.

Ash came in wearing a Santa hat, sweats, and a T-shirt so old and soft it was a miracle it was still holding together. "I brought you a hat."

"Oh, thank you. I was admiring the sparkles before the kids woke up." He put the hat on, realizing suddenly that his head was cold.

"Ho ho ho. All you need is a matching beard. Maybe a pillow under your shirt?" Ash winked at him.

"Ho ho ho, merry Christmas!" He patted his belly, arching his back.

"You went a little overboard, Uncle Santa." Ash leaned against him. "This is amazing."

"Yeah, you and Mom and Dad helped." He wasn't taking credit—or blame—or all of it.

Ash played innocent. "I have no idea what you're talking about. Nothing has *my* name on it."

"Ha. You are the one who had to have the tricycles!"

"I believe those say, 'from Santa' on them. Boys need bikes! Santa is a wise fellow." Ash grinned, looking as happy as the kids would be when they rode them.

"Santa is brilliant."

There were all sorts of goodies for kids, Mama and Dad, the pups, and Ash. It made him feel so good.

Hell, it made him feel ten thousand feet tall.

"I heard something about breakfast? I can smell whatever your mom is making in the kitchen."

"Santa! Santa day!" The sound of the boys' voices came down the stairs from their bedroom, where they were safely behind a baby gate.

They'd figure that out soon enough, but for now, it kept them out of Sammy's room, and mostly out of trouble.

"Uh-oh! Do I hear little boys?" he called.

"Tio! Tio, necesitamos ir a popo!"

"I'm coming!" He didn't hesitate when they needed to hit the bathroom.

"Run, Tio, run!" Ash was right behind him, giggling as they hurried up the stairs.

"Potty train!" He scooped Walt up and Ash got Will, and they sprinted toward the bathrooms.

"Made it!" Ash called from down the hall. Will was very particular, and almost always made it. He didn't like accidents at all.

"So did we!" Bastian couldn't stop laughing, especially when he heard Sammy say, "Boys are gross."

"Merry Christmas, Sammy!" Ash called out.

"Merry Christmas! I'm going down to help make breakfast and see if Santa came!"

"You got lots of coal, I'm sure."

"No, you did!" Sammy laughed, and he could hear her feet on the stairs.

"We'll be down in a second." He grinned at Walt. "You done, buddy?"

"Uh-huh. Santa day!"

He got Walt cleaned up and redressed in his Christmas jammies, and they ran into Will and Ash in the hall. Ash headed down the stairs first and Will and Walt plopped onto their butts and scootched their way down after him.

The boys got down to the bottom, going wide-eyed, but Sammy was crying in her grampa's arms.

Dad gave him a nod, a sad, little smile, and Bastian got it. This was the kids' first Christmas without their folks, and Sammy felt that the most. She had to be free to feel what she felt.

Ash slipped a hand into his and squeezed a little. "Hey. How are you doing?"

"Good. Good, I'm just—Will, get out of the presents." He went to snatch little boys. "Presents after breakfast, right, Sammy?"

He was trying to make as many things familiar as he could.

She nodded. "After." She took a hitching breath and then pushed back from Dad. "I want to go help Granny."

"Cool. I'm going to distract your brothers with the puppies. Holler when y'all are ready for us." Those tears weren't about him. Those tears were about her loss.

Sammy gave Dad a kiss and another quick hug, then ran for the kitchen.

"Tough day," Dad said softly, coming to help with the boys.

"We kind of take whatever comes as it comes." Ash

rubbed his back with one hand. "If you two are good here, I think I'll go see what I can do to help get breakfast on the table."

"We're good."

Bastian handed one twin to Dad. "Let's color in our color books."

"Sisser, kai and kai." Walt's little face was so serious.

"She did cry and cry. She's sad."

Will rolled his eyes. "*Santa* day!"

Dad gave Walt a squeeze. "We can make her happier."

"Happy! All happy!" Walt wiggled, and Dad damn near dropped him.

"Oh ho ho. That was a close one." Dad set Walt down and took his hand and looked at him. "Merry Christmas, son."

"Merry Christmas, Dad. It's right that we're just having the holiday, yeah? This is right?"

The therapist had said so.

"It's right." Dad nodded and sighed. "These kids deserve it. Hell, we deserve it. I guess right doesn't mean easy, though."

"No. No, it doesn't mean easy at all. God knows this is hard." He put a crayon in Will's hand. "But worth it."

"Are you kidding? Look at these beautiful boys. Absolutely worth it."

"Santa is red," Will said with all the authority a three-year-old could muster, coloring in Santa's suit in his coloring book.

"Red!" Walt waved a blue crayon in the air and started coloring away.

Dad laughed. "He's going to be a challenge, that one. He reminds me of you."

"Me?" He winked at his dad. "These guys are going to be my cowboys, all the way."

"And Sammy's going to be an astronaut or something." Dad chuckled in that quiet way he always did. "A space cowboy."

"She's amazing." And he loved her more than he could say. He'd do anything to make sure she was okay.

"Breakfast is ready." Mom stuck her head in. "Sammy is serving. It's beautiful in here. Just wonderful, Bastian."

"Thank you." He thought so too. He thought it looked like he cared. "Boys, are you hungry?"

"Hungee!" The terrible two headed off with matching roars.

"Slow down, fellas!" Dad chased after them.

Mom slipped an arm around his waist as they followed. "I didn't sleep very well last night, but seeing these kids is making it better."

"That's it. That's the best we can do."

The table was filled with pancakes and sausage, a fruit salad, syrup and butter and a bowl of scrambled eggs.

"Woo. Y'all did great!"

"I flipped the pancakes and set the table." Sammy was smiling, but her expression was a mix of emotions.

"This looks amazing." Ash went right to Sammy and gave her a quick hug. "Can I help with something?"

"Let's all eat. The pancakes are hot." Mom got everyone moving and sat down, and Bastian helped get the boys ready to eat.

Ash and Dad started passing dishes and they all had full plates in no time.

"It looks perfect, y'all." Bastian smiled at Sammy. "Merry Christmas."

"Merry Christmas." Sammy smiled back and shrugged her shoulders a little. "Hope you're hungry."

"I am starving! You know my position on pancakes and sausage." He took a big bite, and honestly, they were perfect, thank you, Mom.

The twins dug into their pancakes with both hands as if they hadn't eaten in days. Even Dad was quietly chewing between sips of coffee.

"I'm glad we're all staying put today, have you seen the snow?" Mom picked up her glass of orange juice and sipped it.

"It's just coming down." And there were sleds for all three kids, plus Ash. It should be amazing.

"I love it." Ash scooped some more eggs onto his plate. "I always worry about the animals. I know Bastian says they're fine, but it seems pretty cold."

"Those barns are warm as houses. And the cattle are high altitude, hmm?"

"Don't worry, Uncle Ash. Uncle Bast knows what he's talking about." Sammy gave Ash's knee a pat. "He's a cowboy."

Ash's grin was as bright as the Christmas tree. "He sure is."

"Yes, ma'am. All the way to the bone." And he was damn proud of it.

"So what's the tradition, Sammy?" Ash cut a piece of sausage. "Presents next and then... what? Snowmen?"

"Cocoa and toys?" She shrugged, grinned a little. "I guess the little kids should decide."

The *little* kids. Jesus Christ.

Dad didn't miss a beat. "The little ones can decide, and eventually they will nap and then you can decide, hm?"

"Yeah. Yeah, I can decide. Maybe we'll watch a movie. Maybe we'll start a fire and roast marshmallows…"

"We can do all of that at once," Mom suggested. "Movie, fire, cocoa, and sharing a blanket on that big couch. We'll let the men do the dishes."

Sammy's grin grew wider. "We will?"

Mom nodded and winked at him. "Absolutely. You're in charge of dishes, aren't you, Gramps?"

Dad chuckled and shook his head. "I am King of the dirty dishes."

"That's cool!" Sammy giggled softly. "Grampa, Dish King!"

"King!" the twins echoed.

"I'll help. I'm Knight of packing up leftovers." Ash winked at Sammy.

Bastian snorted. "I could be the Squire of Building Fires."

Ash snorted. "Nobody builds a fire like the Fire Squire."

"You guys are so silly." Sammy rolled her eyes.

"It's Christmas!" He wiggled his ears, crossed his eyes. "We're allowed."

The sound of Sammy and the twins giggling at him was what Christmas was all about.

"Your eyes are going to get stuck that way," Mom said, just like… well, like a mom.

"Yes, Mom." He winked at her, shook his head. "Love you!"

"Love you too, Bast." Mom smiled and sipped her coffee. "How is the bacon? I think it came out perfect. I taught Sammy how to make it in the oven."

"Did you? It's amazing. Is there enough for me to have another serving?" He would eat it if it was awful. Thank God it wasn't.

"We made *so* much." Sammy passed him the plate.

"No such thing as too much bacon." Ash took a big bite of the piece he was holding to prove his point.

Sammy giggled then, and the twins cried, "Santa bacon!"

Walt suddenly climbed down from his chair. and took off. "Santa presents!"

"Whoops. We lost one." Ash went chasing after the boy. Will decided he was done with breakfast, too, and followed after Ash.

"Well. That might be it for breakfast," Mom said dryly.

"Can we leave it on the table and graze, though? It's all so good."

Mom smiled at him. "Of course. There are no rules on Christmas."

"Little help, babe?" Ash called from the den.

"Coming!" He ran, the laughing trailing behind him. "Merry Christmas!"

Ash had Walt under one arm and was holding Will by the back of his pajamas. He got a grin and an eye roll. "They're ready for presents."

"Aren't we all?" He scooped Will up. "Which ones do you think are yours?"

"All them!"

"No," Sammy said with authority as she stepped up beside him. "Not *all*. Geez."

"Right? *Geez*," Ash repeated and buried a grin and a soft laugh against his shoulder.

"Only the ones with Ws, boys. For Will and Walt."

The boys vibrated, little bodies buzzing. "W!"

Ash fingers threaded into his. "Brilliant. Should we let them go?"

"Nope. On the sofa. Sammy can play Santa."

"You heard the cowboy." He and Ash headed for the sofa and wrestled the boys down between them.

Mom and Dad came in together and sat in the comfy chairs on either end of the sofa. "Sammy, did I hear you're playing Santa?"

"I am. I guess." Sammy actually grinned. "Ho ho ho?"

Ash snorted. "You can do better than that, Sammy! Ho ho ho!"

Sammy put her hands on her hips. "Ho ho ho!"

"Mewwy Sisser!" Walt yelled, and Will stood up to clap. "Ho ho ho!"

Ash looked ridiculously pleased with himself. "Now we're channeling Santa."

"We are. Let's pass out the presents!" It was time to get this show on the road.

Sammy stole his Santa hat and put it on her own head, then started passing out presents. She started with the boys, handing them each a box.

They both tore into the paper. Will was methodical and Walt tore with more abandon, but they both got chunky remote-control cars with dinosaurs driving them.

"Car!"

"Dino car!"

"I put the batteries in before I wrapped them," Ash whispered in his ear.

"You are my favorite," he whispered back. "I love you something fierce."

Sammy handed out presents to his folks, too. Dad's new golf putter and the apron he'd made with the kids that had their colorful handprints all over it.

Then she came to them, holding a big rectangular package. "This is from me to you both."

"Oh? Thank you, honey." He held it so Ash could unwrap.

Ash smiled at Sammy, then looked at him as if to ask if he knew what it was. "For us?"

"It's a surprise that I made."

"Oh, wow." Ash opened the paper carefully. "Handmade gifts are the best."

"They so are."

The unwrapping exposed an illustration of him and Ash with wedding rings on, the boys in purple tuxes, and Sammy in a big, poofy green dress. There was a church behind them, and a ton of flowers in every color.

Damn, that was pretty.

"Oh, honey. Look at that. It's gorgeous."

"Oh my god. Sammy, this is so beautiful." Ash held it like it was the Hope Diamond and blinked like he was holding back tears. "Look at our rings! And you look great in green, girlfriend."

"It's gorgeous. Where should we hang it, Ash? In here? On the stairwell? I want everyone to see it."

Sammy beamed at them, her pleasure evident.

"The stairs, so you see when you come in the door. And we need a nice frame, right?" Ash reached over and pulled Sammy in. "We got you some nice presents, but none of them are as nice as this."

"I just—we're family, right?"

"We are. We're family, and we're going to make it, all five of us." He winked at Sammy. "Thanks, girl. It's amazing. I couldn't be more pleased."

And he couldn't be. They were rebuilding one life out of three separate ones, and it was a strong braid of rope.

Not smooth, maybe, but it would take their weight, so long as they held on.

WANT MORE BA & JODI?

Interested in learning more about BA's cowboys and Jodi's gentlemen? Want free fiction and news? Join our newsletters!

What's Up with Jodi

https://readerlinks.com/l/2317334

Spurs and Shifters

https://lp.constantcontact.com/su/A9CRUzp/baandjulia

Hey, Y'all!

We want to thank you for giving Diamonds in the Rough a try. We hope you enjoyed the story.

If you can spare a few minutes to post a review at the retail website where you made your purchase, we'd very much appreciate it!

Don't forget to "like" our Facebook pages and groups to keep up with all the news--new releases, sales announcements, giveaways, sneak peeks-- and of course the rodeo pictures, coffee memes and just general fun. We'd love to have all y'all!

Yeehaw and thanks for reading!

BA & Jodi

ABOUT JODI

JODI takes herself way too seriously and has been known to randomly break out in song. Her queer MCs are imperfect but genuine, stubborn but likable, often kinky, and frequently their own worst enemies. They are characters you can't help but fall in love with while they stumble along the path to their happily ever after. For those looking to get on her good side, Jodi's obsessions include nonfat lattes, basketball (go Celtics!), and tequila any way you pour it.

Website: jodipayne.net

Newsletter: https://readerlinks.com/l/2317334

All Jodi's Social Links: linktr.ee/jodipayne

ABOUT BA

Western to the bone and an unrepentant Daddy's Girl, BA Tortuga spends her days with her hounds and her beloved wife, having mother-daughter dates, and eating Mexican food. When she's not doing that, she's writing. She spends her days off watching rodeo, knitting, and surfing Pinterest in the name of research. Following their own personal joys, BA and Julia heard the call of the high desert and they now live in the New Mexico mountains. BA's personal saviors include her wife, her best friends, and coffee. Lots of coffee. Really good coffee.

Having written everything from fist-fighting cowboys to rural single dads to werewolves, BA does her damnedest to tell the stories of her heart, which is committed to giving everyone their happily ever after. With books ranging from heart-warming stories of found families, to rodeo cowboys that are fighting to make a mark, to fiery passionate love affairs, BA refuses to be pigeon-holed by anyone but the voices in her head.

BA loves to talk to her readers and can be found at http://batortuga.com/ and her newsletter signup link is http://bit.ly/BAJulianews

AVAILABLE FROM JODI & BA

The Cowboy and the Dom Trilogy

First Rodeo, Book One

Razor's Edge, Book Two

No Ghosts, Book Three

The Soldier and the Angel, a Cowboy and Dom Novel

Sin Deep Series

set in The Cowboy and the Dom Universe

Sin Deep

Trouble with Cowboys

East Meets Westerns

(single titles)

<u>Wrecked</u>

Flying Blind

Special Delivery, A Wrecked Holiday Novel

Seeds and Sunshine

Pickup Man

Temptation Ranch

The Merry Everything Series

<u>Window Dressing</u>

Cowboy Protection

Cowboys and Cupcakes

The Higher Elevation Series

Heart of a Cowboy

Land of Enchantment

Keeping Promises

Bigger Than Us

Home Free

The Triskelion Series

Breaking the Rules

Making a Mark

Making the Rules

Les's Bar Series

Just Dex

Hide Bound

Wholly Trinity

New Tricks

The On the Ranch Series

Tending Tyler

Roped In

Diamonds in the Rough

The Collaborations Series

Refraction

Syncopation

Puzzles Series

Cryptic

Summit Springs Sapphic (F/F) Romance

Christmas Bizarre

Honeymoon in the Cards

www.ingramcontent.com/pod-product-compliance
Lightning Source LLC
Chambersburg PA
CBHW072005170726
47999CB00013B/162